terrO.R.

By Joseph J. Neuschatz MD

ISBN-10 1-60145-015-X
ISBN-13 978-1-60145-015-9

Editorial resuscitation by Karri Neuschatz Parola and Tim Brough

Book cover by Lianne Galazka

Booklocker.com, Inc.
2006

Dedications

Thanks to:

My beautiful wife Genia, the creator of a calm and happy family life for this chronically tired anesthesiologist.

My supportive children.

Edward Norris MD who transformed a newly graduated Anesthesiology resident into a practicing physician.

Marvin Ackerman MD for his positive second medico-literary opinion.

Thanks!

Joe

TERRO.R. IS NOTHING BUT

PROMPT, SEVERE, INFLEXIBLE

JUSTICE

Maximilien Robespierre

February 5, 1794 speech

Preface

Unexpected deaths under anesthesia occur almost daily in American operating rooms.

Some remain unexplainable. Until now.

I hope this timely novel is fiction.

one

It had been a much appreciated quiet night, so Philip Newman MD, anesthesiologist, woke up at his usual 5:35 in the morning. Instinctively, he switched off the clock radio before it rang. His sleep was interrupted often enough by the bedside telephone during the nights he was on call. No need for the alarm bonus. Nevertheless, Phil always made sure that the wake-up button was *on* when he went to bed. Nobody can rely 100 percent on internal clocks. Jarring external backups are necessary evils for people who can't afford being late.

Anesthesiologists are commonly called out of bed to provide their services for emergency surgery, help in delivering babies, perform tracheal intubation in poorly breathing newborns, and to attempt the resuscitation of patients in cardiac arrest. However, unlike police officers, firefighters, or ambulance drivers, doctors are not allowed to drive cars equipped with sirens and flashing lights. Even when responding to a life and death *Code Blue,* an anesthesiologist must stop at red lights, respect stop signs and yield to fire trucks. Dr. Newman was lucky: he lived only a mile away from the hospital.

Still clad in his surgical greens, he climbed slowly out of bed. It was not unusual for Dr. Newman to return home and go to bed without changing his hospital scrub suit. Useful time was saved by changing clothes only once, on the return to the operating room. In our days, such a thing is common. You often see doctors and nurses wearing OR garb in the street, in fast food restaurants, in coffee shops and even, like the now famous Dr. Oz, on the Oprah Show.

While shaving, he observed his reflection in the mirror. Few wrinkles, no blemishes. Only the hairline betrayed his 45 years. The balding head harshly reflected the bathroom light as he combed and sprayed his remaining hair to camouflage his scalp. His wife, Kyra, had been prodding him to get rid of this comb-over hairstyle that he had spent the past twenty years mastering.

Washing the leftover shaving cream from his face, Philip smiled. It felt good to have an easy day ahead. Let the younger guys take care of abdominal aortic aneurysms and bowel resections for a change. I've done my share, he thought. Today, he had a bilateral tattoo removal with possible skin grafts, scheduled to take four hours, a rhinoplasty, which like most nose jobs should take no more than ninety minutes, and a two hour bilateral blepharoplasty. The eyelid surgery was his last case. He should be on the tennis courts by 3 PM. Long live plastic surgery!

Phil Newman was a golf school dropout. Tennis was now his all consuming hobby. He had met Kyra during a game of mixed doubles. She was taken by his humorous good nature and by his obvious, almost youthful, infatuation with her. He enshrined her as a beautiful, blonde, tall, intelligent and dedicated pediatric nurse. Marriage followed eight years ago, after only several months of courtship.

Kyra had many of the same characteristics as his first wife did. He had met Susan while in medical school and they got married after only a few months of courtship. Though they hadn't planned it, Susan became pregnant during Phil's anesthesia residency. Sue felt great throughout her pregnancy and went into labor a week before her due date. She gave birth to a handsome curly haired boy they named Jacob, after her father.

It wasn't until Jacob was around five months old that Phil and Susan started to sense that something was wrong with him. Their previously happy, healthy baby had stopped smiling and was pronounced as failing to thrive by their pediatrician. They were referred to a pediatric specialist who made the horrific diagnosis: Tay-Sachs disease. Testing confirmed that Susan and Phil were both carriers of the Tay-Sachs gene and had passed on the genetic death sentence to their son. Jacob had been born without the vital Hex-A enzyme needed for the development of a healthy nervous system. There was no medical recourse.

The next three and half years seemed like a hellish lifetime as they watched despondently as Jacob went blind and deaf, before becoming paralyzed and non-responsive. He died a month before his fourth birthday. Philip and Susan's divorce followed soon after as they both sought to put the horrible event behind them.

Phil discussed openly with Kyra his reasons for not wanting children, the day he proposed. She agreed to keep taking her birth control pills. Kyra worked at the same hospital as Philip, the Soundedge General. However, they went to work in separate cars since he had to examine his first outpatient surgery patient at 6:30 in the morning and reach the operating room suite by 7 AM, to get ready for the 7:30 *incision time.*. Morning shifts for ward nurses began at 8 AM, so Kyra usually prepared breakfast while Phil was in the shower.

Today was like any other non-emergency day: A goodbye kiss to Kyra, an uneventful drive to the hospital. With the driver side's window open, he inserted the parking card in the electronic receptacle. The entrance bar, not broken for a change, opened noiselessly. Most parking spaces reserved for MD's were still available at such an early hour, so he parked near the outpatient surgery entrance, grabbed his stethoscope from the glove compartment and left the car, pressing the key ring button marked *lock*. The Lexus responded noiselessly, by flashing its lights. With his picture ID carefully clipped to his shirt pocket, Philip Newman, MD opened the hospital door, ready to start another day.

It irked Newman that more and more operations were being performed on a *same day surgery* basis. Possibly good for a patient's morale, probably better for the HMO's cash registers, but not so great for anesthesiologists. He couldn't help but nervously wonder if all patients respected the *NPO after MN* (nothing by mouth after midnight) order. How tempting it must be to grab a quick cup of java on the way to the hospital? Under anesthesia, that coffee could cause vomiting, regurgitation, aspiration, pneumonia, or even death. And how precise is a supposedly complete detailed medical history taken under stress, minutes before surgery? How frequently do medications taken that morning go unmentioned? How often dangerous non-prescription herbal supplements are not considered relevant?

Nora, the admitting clerk, welcomed him with a forced smile. "Good morning, Dr. Newman. Which room?"

"Morning, Nora. I'm in the plastic surgery room. Is my first victim in?" Hoping to establish a light mood, Newman's attempts to create spontaneous humor were a mixture of success and failure. His approach was usually not much different than that used by other congenial physicians. During the non existent *Weapons of Mass Destruction* (WMD) episode in Iraq, he adapted to the daily news by sometimes introducing himself as "Philip Newman, MD – medical doctor, not mass destructor." Later, when visiting awakening patients in the post anesthesia care unit, his "Welcome to the recovery paradise! Everything went great! My name is Saint Peter," usually passed over the heads of everyone in the recovery room, including the bleary eyed patients.

Nora checked the computer. "Let's see...tattoo removal with possible skin graft, Doctor Maloney surgeon, patient James Walker - prepped and ready to go in holding booth number three."

"Thanks, Nora." Grabbing one of the multiple *Soundedge General Hospital, Port Lincoln, Long Island, New York* ball point pens from the coffee mug on Nora's desk, he walked over to booth number three and pushed the curtain aside, enough to allow him to enter. "Good morning, Mister Walker! I'm the gas-passer. Your sandman. My name is Doctor Newman." Seeing the puzzled look on the young man's face, he added 'the anesthesiologist."

"Good morning," came a double reply. The young man, dressed in a hospital gown, was sitting on the bed, and a middle-aged man, evidently his father, sat on a chair next to him.

Dr. Newman took the patient's chart from the chart holder and began to read: "Let's see, James Walker, 19 years old, no medical history, no allergies, on no medications, no previous surgery, non-smoker, non-alcohol drinker, no drugs and...nothing to eat or drink since midnight...is all this correct?"

"Yeah."

"I see you both signed the surgical consent. It wasn't necessary. You're over eighteen."

"My father insisted," he grumbled.

"OK. Please open the gown. I have to listen to your chest."

Tattoos, long hair, thick beard, mumbling accession to parental dominance...typical rebellious teenager, versus exasperated, clean-cut parent, mused the doctor. Been there, seen that before, he added unconsciously, and then scratched his head trying to resolve a bit of déjà vu. This kid looks familiar. Who does he remind me of?

"It says here that you had both arms tattooed only six months ago. Why the removal now?" Newman inquired.

Momentary silence. Then the young man's gaze shifted to the middle-aged man who gave a disapproving glance and took over. "He came home tattooed after a trip abroad. There will be no tattoos in my family. I'm his father."

4

This is no typical affluent suburban family squabble, opined Newman to himself, somewhat taken aback. The father decidedly holds the reins in this family. None of the laissez-faire attitude here. And yet, how did the kid get away with all the trappings of rebellion in the first place? Newman replaced suspicions with reality. Hey, it's none of my business. They want surgical removal and they need anesthesia. Who am I to ask questions? What they need, is my business. Philip dismissed everything as *just the way things are today*, and then proceeded to listen to the patient's heart and lungs.

Everything seemed okay. Charted blood pressure 110/70. Respiration 16. Temperature, hemoglobin and urinalysis, all within normal limits. The pulse did seem a bit fast at 112, but not unusual. Young outpatients not receiving pre-op sedation tended to show higher pulses during the stressful pre-operative period. Inpatients arriving to the OR sedated, tended to have lower pulses and be calmer.

"Okay, let's talk about what we are going to do. You have a choice between general anesthesia and a local anesthetic with intravenous sedation. In simpler operations, the general anesthesia could be administered by mask, but not in your case. Your beard makes it impossible to achieve a tight fit. Some anesthetic gases will leak around the mask, instead of all going in your lungs. I would therefore have to intubate you, which means that I must place a tube inside your windpipe, after you're asleep. This puts any loose teeth or any fragile dental caps you may have in jeopardy and could also leave you with a sore throat after the operation. Unless, of course, you agree and sign a consent, to have your beard removed."

"Please don't touch my beard!" The young man appeared panicky. "I already talked to Dr. Maloney about the anesthesia. He told me that you would make me a little sleepy with something you give in my vein and he would inject a local anesthetic with some other stuff which would keep me comfortable longer."

" Epinephrine?"

"Yeah. That's what I think he said... epinephrine!"

"OK, Jim. May I call you Jim?"

James Walker nodded condescendingly.

"No problem! We won't touch your beard. I promise! Now, let me explain to you what is going to happen inside the operating room. I'll have to stay as far as possible from your tattooed arms. Your arms will become sterile surgical fields. This forces me to start your intravenous infusion in one of your legs or feet, and use your other leg to check the blood pressure. You'll receive oxygen through a small tube in the nose, and you'll be attached to an EKG machine and a skin thermometer. I'll use a precordial stethoscope on your chest to listen to your heartbeats, and a pulse oximeter attached to your earlobe to measure the oxygen saturation in your bloodstream. Any questions?"

"How long will it take, doctor?" Walker queried.

"You're asking the wrong guy. That's up to the surgeon. It all depends on whether Dr. Maloney finds it necessary to do skin grafts."

"I see..."

Newman wrote his preoperative notes on the back of the anesthesia record, which was already on the chart. Once the notes were signed, he lifted his head to face the father. "Okay, Mr. Walker. They're going to bring your son to the operating room in a wheelchair. An orderly will show you to the waiting room. I'm going in to get ready. As soon as we're done, Dr. Maloney and I will come talk to you."

While walking toward the OR's locker room to change into a fresh scrub suit, Newman reviewed his findings. Both tattoos were smaller than he expected. No need for skin grafts. The case will be much shorter than four hours. Soon after the first incision, he would tell the circulating nurse to call the admitting office and ask them to move up his next two patients. He might make it to the tennis court by one!

two

The men's locker room was already busy. Nick, one of the orderlies, was arranging clean scrub suits on the linen shelves. Upper shelves: shirts, lower shelves: pants. From left to right, the sizes: small, medium, large and extra large. Mike, another orderly, was emptying dirty laundry bags. Only scrub suits and some of the drapes and towels are washable and reusable. Everything else: masks, shoe covers, surgical caps, most drapes, most towels and even the nail brushes are thrown away...all part of our modern disposable society.

Jay McMullen, the talented latest addition and youngest anesthesiologist in the group, was politely listening to Joe Rosenberg, a vascular surgeon. Joe had arrived early, in order to insert pre-op arterial lines in a patient scheduled for an arterial bypass. But his tendency to be somewhat logorrheic and pompous often led to an irritating schedule delay. Since that frightening day when he had saved the life of a man oozing blood internally following repair of an aortic dissection, he had acquired the nickname *The Wizard of Ooze.*

Rosenberg was probably the only Soundedge surgeon who knew his nickname and was proud of it. On the other hand, nobody had the guts to tell Norman Kramer, the diminutive and pompous orthopedic surgeon, that behind his back he was known as *Napoleon Bones-Apart.*

Phil removed his shoes, changed into *clean greens,* then put his shoes back and covered them with paper covers and his head with a paper cap. Following that, he grabbed a surgical mask and attached it to his forehead, just like miners attach their lamps: mask in front, rubber band behind. After washing his hands with liquid soap and water, he dried them on paper towels and moved the mask so as to cover his mouth and nose. Time to go to work.

In room two, Linda Burns the scrub nurse, was carefully opening the sterile instruments onto sterile trays. They exchanged polite "good mornings," from behind their masks. Robert Raye, a tall, slender Marine Corps veteran and ex-Vietnam medic, was the circulating nurse. "Can I bring him in, Phil?" asked Robert.

Unlike some of the other doctors at the Soundedge hospital, Newman liked to be on a first name basis with all his coworkers: "In a couple of minutes, Bob. Give me a chance to check my instruments and mix my solutions."

Philip changed the *soda lime*, an important carbon dioxide absorber in the breathing circuit, checked the anesthesia machine for possible leaks, inspected the automatic ventilator, arranged his instruments, tubes and airways and made sure that the laryngoscope light was working. Now satisfied that everything was ready to go, he made up a diluted solution of Propofol, a short acting intravenous anesthetic, using a syringe and needle. The bag of saline in which he injected the medication turned white. Newman preferred this anesthetic, especially for outpatient cases. He liked to call it *Milk of Amnesia*. Finally, he made sure to attach a long, extended IV tube to the insertion spigot of the bag.

"OK, Bob. I'm ready. Bring the patient in. Don't forget to double check his chart."

Linda intervened. "Before you go, Bob, please open the Lidocaine with Epi."

"One or two percent?"

"For local anesthesia, Dr. Maloney uses 2% Lidocaine with 1/100000 Epi, if the patient is not allergic to it."

Newman heard the conversation. "I checked. He denies allergies."

Robert carefully opened two 50 c.c. vials labeled "2% Lidocaine with 1/100000 adrenaline" and poured them slowly, directly into the sterile metallic bowl held by Linda's gloved hands. Epinephrine and adrenaline are different names for the same medication. The name *epinephrine* is preferred in the OR abbreviated lingo. It's easier to say *Epi*, than *Adren*. After discarding the now empty vials in the recycling receptacle, Robert left to bring the patient. Linda began filling up five 20 cc. syringes with the local anesthetic.

"Morning, Phil, Linda." Jesse Maloney, 54-year-old plastic surgeon, made his appearance walking backwards, scrubbed, masked, wet arms up in the air. He pushed the OR door open with his backside.

"Morning Doc." Linda immediately handed him a sterile towel. Once his arms were dry, he put them through the sleeves of a sterile gown she held open. The used towel was discarded on the floor to be picked up later by the circulating nurse.

"Hi, Jesse," said Newman. "Let me help you tie your gown. Bob is getting the patient." Holding one end of the sterile waistband, Jesse Maloney made a 360-degree turn. His pelvis and torso were now completely covered by the gown. Phil grabbed one end of the belt from Jesse and the other from Linda. While he was doubling the knot behind the no longer sterile back of Maloney, the OR door reopened. It was the young patient in a wheelchair, medical chart on his knees, pushed from behind by Bob Raye.

"Are you ready, young man?" asked Maloney, busy inserting a pair of grossly non-surgical hands into a pair of extra-large surgical gloves held open for him by Linda.

"As ready as I can be. You know very well that it wasn't my idea to have this operation."

"That's true. Next time ask for your father's permission before you do stupid things!"

Newman, head bent down to recheck his anesthesia tray, smiled briefly to himself. Typical Maloney – tell it like it is. Satisfied, he looked up again, only to observe the bearded Walker silently mouthing something. Was he fuming and trying to answer back? Was he chewing gum? His mouth was now masticating and making swallowing movements. *Petit mal* seizure? "Are you okay Jim? I hope you're not eating something. Are you?"

Walker was trying to get up from his wheelchair with Bob Raye's assistance. "Yeah, I'm fine. Just trying to swallow some saliva. My mouth is real dry."

"It's common, very common Jim, to feel dry when you've had nothing to drink for a while. You're a little dehydrated. I'll give you all the fluids you need in the vein, during the surgery."

Raye helped his patient settle on the operating room table, face up, gown removed, arms extended on towel covered armboards. The tattoos were now visible in all their beauty: colorful flame exhaling dragons. After the circulating nurse covered Walker's pelvic area with a surgical sheet, he attached a loose safety belt over patient's abdomen and, turning toward the anesthesiologist, asked: "Need help, Phil?"

"I'd appreciate. Dr. Maloney is not completely ready," Newman replied.

Robert Raye placed a blood pressure cuff on the patient's right leg while Newman tightened a tourniquet on the left. "Thank you, Bob. Just put the EKG leads on. You have other things to do. I'll take care of the rest." The ex-Vietnam medic attached the EKG and went on to prep the patient's arms with antiseptic wash, followed by iodine swab. The right arm was left exposed for immediate surgery while the left one was wrapped in sterile towels.

Phil took advantage of the time necessary for the left foot veins to become more visible. He placed an oxygen cannula in patient's nostrils and started a 4-liter/minute-oxygen flow. Next, he squeezed a temperature probe under Walker's left shoulder and read the results: skin temperature 97. Now, all Philip had left to do was fasten the diaphragm of a stethoscope next to patient's left nipple with double-stick tape and attached the pulse oximeter probe to his left earlobe. The blood pressure read 138/82, the pulse was 116 and regular, the EKG reading was fast but the tracing was normal. The oxygen saturation was 100%. Maybe James Walker is more anxious than he appears to be, thought Phil while attaching the draped anesthesia screen, to separate the sterile and non-sterile areas.

Sufficiently satisfied with the patient's readings, the anesthesiologist went to observe the left foot. The veins seemed big enough for a #18 intracath. After cleaning the skin with an alcohol sponge, he inserted the large needle without a hitch. Walker moaned, but didn't move. Assured by the return of blood that he was in the right place, Phil pushed the plastic catheter into the vein over the needle, removed the needle and threw it inside a *Sharps box,* the container for the disposing of biohazardous materials. After attaching the long IV tubing to the catheter, he secured everything in place with adhesive tape, and removed the tourniquet. "Ready, Jesse?"

"Go ahead, Phil. Have a good rest, Mr. Walker. Is the local ready, Linda?"

Picking up one of the five syringes, Linda Burns nodded yes. Then she asked, "What size needles, Dr. Maloney?"

"Make them 22's."

Newman opened the intravenous drip. "Please count backwards from 100 Jim." By "78," the mumble was unintelligible. Phil slowed the drip down to a trickle and checked the vital signs: blood pressure 132/80, oxygen saturation 100, and pulse 112. Things were calming down. "Go ahead, Jesse!"

Maloney began injecting the local anesthetic with epinephrine. "I'm 99% sure that I won't have to graft him." He turned his head toward Bob. "Could you call admitting and ask them to move my other patients up?"

"Yes, Sir!" responded the ex-Marine.

Newman smiled widely behind his paper mask. What a day! No worry about being on time for tennis. Maloney had taken care of everything.

three

The cardioscope was showing a fast but regular sinus rhythm. Philip made the customary abbreviated entries on the anesthesia record, *RSR...RSR* and marked down all other monitored information (pulse, blood pressure, temperature, etc). Boring but important liability prevention. The daily red tape of an anesthesiologist.

About 15 minutes into the operation, Phil observed a premature ventricular contraction, an unexpected strangely shaped squiggle on the cardioscope screen, very different from the *RSR*. He checked the blood pressure in a hurry: 140/86. One single *PVC* is usually no big deal. However, the pulse was also going up. It was now 134, higher than the first reading on patient's arrival in the OR. The oxygen saturation was unchanged. A second *PVC* soon appeared, followed by a third.

From his six foot two height, Maloney observed the changes in his anesthesiologist and the disappearance of the relaxed atmosphere behind the anesthesia screen. "What's going on, Phil?"

"I don't know, Jesse, but I don't like it. We had a few premature ventricular contractions on his EKG. I hate unexplainable *PVC*'s in a young healthy patient with absolutely no history of cardiac disease. Maybe it's due to the Epi?"

"The epinephrine? Yeah, you're probably right. Should I continue the surgery?"

"Please continue, but only if you don't inject anymore of the local with epi until I tell you. How much did he use so far, Linda?"

The scrub nurse checked her syringes, "46 cc's, Phil."

The *PVC*s became more and more frequent. The plastic surgeon worked faster and faster, trying to finish the removal of the tattoo from the left arm.

Patients often exhibit a premature heartbeat known as an *extrasystole* when surgeons are pulling on bowels or other internal organs and the excitable vagus nerve produces a *vagal reflex*. But a *vagal reflex* during tattoo removal? In desperation, Newman injected 0.4 mg of intravenous Atropine Sulfate, the antidote for such reflexes. It was to no avail. Instead of the expected acceleration of the heart rate and normalization of the EKG tracing, the *PVC*s became more frequent. Soon, each normal beat was followed by a premature one. Newman reached for the cardioscope to increase the sound volume... beep, BEEP...beep, BEEP...beep, BEEP...

Maloney looked at the cardioscope screen. "What's going on Phil? *Bigemini?*"

"Yeah! Stop the surgery!" Newman replaced the Propofol solution with a 5% dextrose-in-water bag. "Get the crash cart in the room, STAT! Bob, call *Code Blue!*"

Newman removed the anesthesia screen and used his surgical mask to wipe his forehead before throwing the now wet mask into a bucket. It's easy to forget important cardiopulmonary resuscitation steps when under pressure and Phil knew it. Usually, he only helped other doctors with their CPR's and regularly trained on *Resusci-Anne* the CPR teaching doll. But his own patient in cardiac distress? This was uncommon. Thank God for that brainwashing alphabetical training!

A for *AIRWAY*.

Inject a quick 100 mm of succynilcholine into the now temporarily wide-open IV tubing to help paralyze the patient and allow tracheal intubation.

Phil ventilated the unresponsive, unconscious patient as well as he could with 100% oxygen by mask. As soon as the neck muscles stopped fasciculating, indicating that his jaw was relaxed, he opened his mouth to illuminate the vocal cords with the laryngoscope. Hastily, he introduced a number 8 cuffed endotracheal tube in the windpipe, and then quickly inflated the cuff with an air syringe to prevent leaks. After connecting the endotracheal tube to the anesthesia hoses, he exposed the chest.

B for *BREATHING*.

Squeezing the black rubber anesthetic bag to force oxygen into the lungs, Phil watched the satisfactory up and down movement of the chest and listened with his stethoscope to both lungs, before turning on the automatic ventilator.

The massive stainless steel crash cart was now in the room. Peggy Kane, the 40-year-old OR supervisor, came in through a side door. Linda covered the unfinished surgery site with a sterile towel. Mask and gloves off, Jesse Maloney was ready to help. The bigeminal rhythm continued...beep, BEEP...beep, BEEP...beep, BEEP...

Phil injected 100 milligrams of 100% Lidocaine into the IV tubing and let the intravenous drip run fast again. Lidocaine, the local anesthetic, also has a calming effect on irritable heart muscles.

The automatic blood pressure machine showed a sudden drop: 72/48. Pulse 188, O2 saturation 72, lips getting bluish. Bad sign! He pushed the button again: 58 over nothing! Darn!

C for *CIRCULATION*.

"Start cardiac massage, Jesse! The pressure is going down to zero!"

"Drop the table, Phil.," Maloney replied.

Phil pressed the pedal at the OR table base with his right foot to lower it. Standing on the left side of the comatose patient, Maloney started pushing on his chest, right hand over left and counting "one, one thousand...two, one thousand... three, one thousand..." to simulate a regular cardiac massage rhythm. After "five, one thousand," he took a short break to allow Philip, who had gone back to manual ventilation, to inflate the lungs with oxygen. The counting restarted, "one, one thousand...two, one thousand..."

An electrocardioscope is useless when performing chest compressions. Newman knew the importance of checking the scope during respiratory pauses. In the beginning, the tracing simply indicated tachyarrhythmia, a rapid irregular heart. But now, after inspecting all the wires to make sure they were still connected, he was dismayed to observe a classical ventricular fibrillation pattern. The heartbeat and pulse were out of sync.

D for *DRUGS*.

"Bob! Epi and sodium bicarb, IV STAT!" The Marine veteran knew how to execute orders. He administered the ready-to-use medications within seconds. His calm assurance was almost unnatural. For someone who treated blown-apart soldiers in Vietnam, what's an unexpected cardiac arrest?

E for...?

What in the world does E stand for? Phil hesitated, but quickly remembered.

E for *ELECTROCARDIOGRAM*.

The patient was already attached to the machine. But not having a printed record in the chart at a time like this, could come back to haunt you.

"Linda, start the graph please. Mark on the paper the time for each medication given. Jesse, stop the massage for a few seconds. Let's get some undisturbed tracing."

Linda and Jesse complied. They knew that during a CPR, the anesthesiologist is in command. The EKG paper started rolling out, like an oversized ticker tape. Phil glanced at the printed tracing. No doubt...ventricular fibrillation!

F for *FIBRILLATION*.

"Peggy, the defibrillator. Jesse, resume the massage."

Giving orders to Peggy Kane made Phil feel uneasy. It's hard enough having to work with an ex-mistress who hates you. But giving her orders? The OR supervisor spread skin-contact jelly on the defibrillating paddles. She was the only person in the room still wearing a mask. "An old antiseptic nursing school habit," was always her explanation. Philip remembered teasing her once, "Bullshit Peg! I call it vanity! The mask emphasizes your beautiful eyes and hides your wrinkles! It makes you look like a gorgeous and mysterious TV nurse." He instantly regretted the "hides your wrinkles" comment but she had just ignored his words.

"Ready?" Peggy inquired.

"Ready." Maloney removed his hands from Walker's chest. Newman disconnected the hoses from the endotracheal tube. With the exception of Kane, everybody took a backward step. Peggy put the paddles on the patient's chest. The anesthesiologist counted, "three, two, one...SHOOT!"

Bob Raye pressed the blinking defibrillator button. Walker's body jerked, as if he was trying to get off the operating room table. During this time, the cardioscope tracing was unreadable. Phil waited for the tracing to retake its place in the middle of the screen. Darn! Still ventricular fibrillation.

"Epi, cardiac massage, Bicarb. Get ready to shock him again!" ordered Newman. He checked Walker's lips and fingernails. They looked bluish, but under artificial OR lights, color changes are always accentuated.

G for *GASES*.

"Quick, call the lab, Linda. I need blood gases STAT!" After reconnecting the hose to the endotracheal tube, Phil started squeezing the bag again.

"Five, one thousand..." Maloney took a short break. He checked the cardioscope tracing for a second. Pulling on the funnel shaped OR light, the surgeon brought the powerful beam above Walker's glassy eyes to observe the pupils. They were dilated and not responding. "We're losing him, Phil. Maybe we should quit?"

"Not yet, Jesse. You must be exhausted, I know. Let me take over. I'm putting him back on automatic ventilation." Phil went over to the left side of the table. The sweating Maloney sat dripping on the vacated anesthesiologist's chair. Phil restarted the massage energetically. No point to open the chest, he thought. Open cardiac massages are not indicated when patients don't respond to CPR.

Peggy Kane checked the flashing orange button. "The defibrillator is recharged." She lifted the paddles. "Ready...move back, Phil!"

four

Mary Brown, the past-her-prime-pleasantly plump OR secretary, spent most of her working hours on the phone. The job wasn't easy, but Mary was good at it. She knew how to juggle two telephones, four extension lines, and eight intercoms better than anybody else. "It must be easier to tame a Barnum and Bailey lion," she liked to joke, "than to put the chief of surgery on hold." Her job description read "8 AM to 4 PM," but she always made her daily appearance, coffee in hand, just after 7:30 in the morning. Today was no different. She was already at her post, telephone receiver in hand, two calls on hold, and an untouched styrofoam cup of black-no-sugar on her desk, when the buzzer started buzzing and the intercom alarm light began to flash. "I will have to put you on hold," she said to her invisible caller, "something is going on in room two."

She had transferred from a desk job in the records room to her desk job in the operating room on her own request. The always increasing surgical load, finally convinced the hospital administration to replace part-time volunteers, the *pink ladies,* with a full-time secretary. "If I'm going to spend eight hours a day sitting on my butt," Mary declared the day she applied for transfer, "I would rather spend them talking to people. Another year in the records room and I'll be talking to microfilms!"

Today, she was no longer sure she'd made the right move. Her old position meant boredom for sure, but it also meant regular coffee breaks and few interruptions. The new job was nothing but interruption on top of interruption. New tensions added to existing ones. Everything was important. Everything had to be done *now.*

Outside each operating room was a lighted buzzer operated from inside by a foot pedal. If the circulating nurse was busy prepping the patient and the surgeon or the scrub nurse needed something from outside, the foot pedal allowed for the ringing of the buzzer without the contamination of sterile gloved hands. Each time the pedal was pressed, the light flashed both outside the room and on Mary Brown's intercom panel. For routine calls, the pedal was pressed for one, or maximum two

17

buzzes. Non stop buzzing signified *Code Blue,* the dreaded, and no longer secret, hospital code phrase for cardiac arrest.

An OR secretary quickly learns that, thank God, most alarms are false alarms. Perhaps medical students observing an operation had inadvertently pressed on the pedal while leaning against the wall, or an absentminded surgeon had neglected to turn off the buzzer after making an outside request. During her six months on the job, Mary could recall only one real *Code,* but at least two dozen false alarms. Why didn't they install a separate panic button in each room? Why was it so important to remain sterile while a patient was dying? Sometimes she wished she had the guts to ask this kind of questions.

The buzzing and the flashing continued. How much longer should she wait? Only last week, Mary had been reprimanded by the unpredictable Peggy Kane for crying wolf too soon. Defensively, she checked the day's schedule on the computer: room two. Time: 7:30 AM, Patient: James Walker, Age: 19. Operation: removal of tattoos from both arms with possible skin grafts. surgeon: Jesse Maloney. anesthesiologist: Philip Newman. It must be a false alarm, she decided.

But the alarm did not stop. Time to act! Mary's urgent voice was heard loud and clear throughout the entire surgical suite *"Code Blue,* **room two!** *Code Blue,* **room two!"**

Within seconds, green clad people appeared from everywhere: nurse's lounge, doctor's lounge, and supply rooms. The stainless steel crash cart went flying towards room two. After the cart went in, the OR supervisor appeared at the door and sent everybody back, to where they came from. She was in charge. There was enough help inside.

Realizing that her telephone was ringing, Mary made an effort to cut loose from the scary but fascinating drama taking place one glass door away. Clearing her throat, she quickly regained her unemotional, professional voice. "operating room, Mrs. Brown..."

A booming voice jolted her ear drum. "Don't you dare to put me on hold again! What are you people doing?! Playing with yourselves?!" Recognizing the unpleasant voice of Norman *Napoleon Bones-Apart* Kramer, Mary was furious. How dare he speak to her like that? Tossing the receiver, she watched it hit the styrofoam cup, but remained motionless when the pool of steaming black coffee splashed on her OR books. She looked at the soaked files while rubbing her eyes, like after a bad dream. What in the world was she doing here? Was this a good place for a secretarial career? A lime-green windowless room with fluorescent lights and a scratched desk, a glass door through which she watched a daily parade of patients, a bunch of egotistical doctors, and the temperamental Peggy Kane?

The coffee dripped on the floor. She needed new coffee. Grabbing her purse from the open desk drawer, Mary Brown bolted to the coffee shop on the main floor.

Soundedge General Hospital was a modern six-floor red brick and dark glass building, built on an elevated piece of land in Port Lincoln, one of the fastest growing communities on Long Island's North Shore. The main lobby was a contemporary delight. A white, round, centrally located information desk manned by two *candy stripers* was surrounded by four groups of six black leather chairs with white Lucite magazine racks in between. The northern wall had three 8 x 8 windows overlooking Long Island Sound. In the middle of the opposite wall, two sliding glass doors marked the main entrance. A uniformed security guard stood watch, as an aide returned from the parking lot, pushing a wheelchair.

A limo was stopped in the circular *No Parking* driveway. Next to it, a *pink lady* talked with two very well dressed couples. Another fund raising guided tour, mused Mary, annoyed. Her mind wandered. In no way would her homely lime-green office be part of the tour. Hospital administrators put their money where eyes can see the results. The OR office could hardly be considered a PR showcase. Maybe, she smiled inwardly, this is the real reason why operating suites are off-limits to the public. Maybe the *STERILE AREA* sign was just an excuse.

The coffee shop was a large enclave, located in the eastern wing of the main lobby. Mary sat on one of the high stools near the counter and ordered black coffee. Her decision was made: quit the OR and wait here until 9 AM when the personnel office opens. She wanted her old job back. Talking to microfilms didn't seem so awful anymore. She glanced at the clock on the left wall. Plenty of time, she thought, 14 minutes before 9:00. This ex-operating room secretary was now going to relax and enjoy her coffee for a change.

five

The alphabetical *Code Blue* training manual ends with the letter G for *GASES*. Maybe somebody should change that? Maybe we should lengthen the list by one more letter? Make it end with the letter H for *HOME*? After all, no matter what the final result of a CPR was, the doctors and the nurses involved, unwaveringly end up going home. Philip wished that the patients could be as lucky.

Instead of trying to serve aces on the tennis court, Newman was now somber and depressed, trying to comprehend what just happened. Had it been a mistake to allow Peggy Kane to become an important part of the CPR crew ? After all, from her position of ex-mistress, she despised him. She once told Kyra, "Your guy chose me to be the one to have fun with before he married you!" Had her lack of team spirit hampered the *Code Blue* team?

The unsuccessful resuscitation attempt of James Walker took the entire morning and then some. Dr. Maloney's two other cases were postponed for another day. The decision to pronounce a healthy young man dead is excruciating. One last futile attempt has to be made, as soon as the previous futile attempts have failed. Precise medical rules always teach when to start the reviving maneuvers, never when to end them. Stories of miraculous returns from the dead are rare, but they do exist. And to make things worse, Jesse Maloney chose to not get too involved. He left the final call in Newman's hands. After all, he was just a plastic surgeon.

During the time Bob Raye prepared the body for the journey to the morgue, Newman kept busy recording the minute-to-minute logs and decisions on the anesthesia record. Now the family and medical examiner had to be notified. Newman's thoughts filled with dread at the thought of talking to the father. Informing next of kin is never easy, but in the case of a seemingly healthy nineteen year old, it was unthinkable.

The father of the deceased, who was asked to move from the waiting area to a private family room, was quietly awaiting to hear from the doctors. When the anesthesiologist and the surgeon arrived, Walker Sr.

was sitting down in a leather armchair, a *Newsweek* on his lap. He placed the magazine on a nearby table and stood up to shake hands.

The man's emotionless reaction to the horrible news was disturbing. His stony face remained still during the entire explanation. Nothing moved. He showed no expression of sorrow, no tears. Numbed, he appeared to accept the events with fated resignation. "Did he suffer?" was his first question. He seemed to accept the negative answer with profound relief. "Why did I insist to have those stupid tattoos removed? Will there be an autopsy? I would like you to know that I'm opposed to it. For religious reasons."

Newman explained that a post-mortem examination could be important, to help them understand what happened. But such decisions are in the hands of the medical examiner. Usually, if the family is opposed to a forensic examination, for personal, religious or other reasons, and if there are no signs of foul play, the county pathologist will not insist on an autopsy.

"I will call him as soon as I leave here and I'll inform him of your wishes," assured Newman.

"Thank you, Doctor."

Phil left the room, leaving Maloney there to finish the conversation. He was convinced that the ME would not perform an autopsy.

Just like any other physician, forensic practitioners carry medical liability insurance to protect against lawsuits. Over the years, coroners have found themselves dragged to court for many different reasons. But the number one justification for litigation remains *mental trauma:* the performing of post mortem examinations against the wishes of next of kins. When the deceased's family objects and there is no evidence of physical injuries or drugs, autopsies are usually skipped. A prudent medical examiner will call it a *fatal heart attack* when a person dies in a hotel room or an *anesthetic death* if the lethal event took place in the operating room. Case closed.

The call to the county coroner was swift. The pathologist listened to what Phil had to say and promised to respect the family wishes. But he did need a copy of the chart for his records.

It was just like Newman expected. medical examiners make the diagnosis of a *anesthetic death,* on the phone, probably without batting an eyelash. And why shouldn't they? After all, even when they do end up performing post mortem examinations on operating room fatalities, the exact cause of death rarely becomes apparent.

In two almost identical cases in which a best selling author, Olivia Goldsmith and a physician's wife, Susan Malitz, died one month apart at the prestigious Manhattan Eye, Ear and Throat Hospital during cosmetic surgery performed under Lidocaine/epinephrine local anesthesia and supplemented by intra-venous sedation, there was no clear conclusion on the cause of death. Just bad luck? It was as if lightning had struck twice in the same spot.

Philip has repeatedly read the New York Times treatises describing these infamous cases. Many practicing anesthesiologists must have done the same thing by now. Written by two investigative reporters, the article was scary but instructive. The pages were still in the glove compartment of his Lexus, left there for future perusing. He removed them one more time, to reread the highlighted paragraphs:

But while the reports detail mistakes and failings in patient care, neither the city nor the state has made a declarative finding about what caused the two deaths, frustrating doctors who are eager to know what changes they should make to protect patients.

"What's the most unusual thing, there's no answer," said Dr. Carroll B. Lesesne, a plastic surgeon at the hospital. "After all these investigations, neither the doctors, the hospital nor the government agencies have come out and said, 'This is what caused it. Everybody is worried. Could it happen to us?"

Since the deaths, some Manhattan plastic surgeons said, patients have become more probing about the risks. Robert C. Silich, a plastic surgeon at New York-Presbyterian Hospital, described the impact on his practice as 'tremendous.'

It's about time for today's surgeons to learn that anesthesia and surgery are different ball games, Newman mused. Since early times, their medical specialty has been divided into two categories: "major surgery" and "minor surgery." Let the entire world know that undergoing anesthesia always represents a major risk. There is no such thing as "minor anesthesia."

According to rumors, Olivia Goldsmith underwent the cosmetic procedure at her literary agent's insistence *to look younger for her next book cover*. What a waste of human life! What was the exact cause of her death? What was the exact cause of James Walker's death? Maybe some dietary supplements? Perhaps he was taking Ephedra, the stimulant containing the banned chemical ephedrine?

Ephedrine quells fatigue, helps with weight loss and boosts performance. But it also increases the blood pressure and accelerates the pulse, stressing the heart. Class actions started by law firms claim that Ephedra containing dietary products have led to strokes, heart attacks, seizures and death.

Ephedra is no longer a legal over-the-counter medication, but Ephedra leftovers are probably present in many medicine and bathroom medicine cabinets. The nutritional supplement was once sold under brand names like *Ripped Fuel* and *Metabolife 356*, marketed to appeal to both desperate dieters trying to shed a few pounds and aspiring young athletes attempting to boost their energy.

In its time, the mysterious demise of Steve Bechler, a 23 year old Baltimore Oriole pitcher, raised many such questions and offered no clear answers. A medical examiner said at the time that it was *probable* that Bechler used a product containing ephedrine and that this product contributed to his death. A bottle of an Ephedra supplement was found in his locker. The word *probable* is one of the medical examiner's favorite expressions when trying to explain a human demise.

Ephedra was also a product taken by people obsessed with their looks. And who are vainer than cosmetic surgery patients? Did the Manhattan Eye, Ear and Throat Hospital investigators look into an Ephedra link? And if Ephedra alone could kill, imagine the fatal interaction between ephedrine and epinephrine? Maybe the young Walker didn't want to admit that he took athletic performance boosters, in front of his father? Could medical examiners differentiate between the surgical epinephrine found in the patient's blood and the Ephedra he possibly took? Chances are this was an impossible undertaking.

Phil put the key in the ignition and started the car. He looked at his watch. My God! Already 5:00 in the afternoon! Almost eleven hours since he left the house this morning! This time, the mile between the hospital and the house seemed to never end.

Kyra, was already at home and preparing supper. She ran into the garage when she heard its automatic door opening. As soon as Newman was out of his car, Kyra hugged him for a prolonged period, without saying a word. After removing her arms from around his neck, she looked at him with her beautiful eyes and said, "I'm really sorry, Phil. It's awful!"

In a good hospital, bad news travels fast.

six

Newman spent an agonizing night, wishing he could stop thinking. Moving around and turning incessantly did not help. Prone, supine or in a fetal position, made no difference. He was still totally awake. Finally, pillow in hand, he tiptoed out of the bedroom, softly closing the door behind him. At least Kyra will get some sleep, he hoped.

It was too late now to take a sleeping pill. He had to be back to work in a few hours. Back to work, like nothing happened. Shower, shave, eat breakfast, drive the car, park the car, and make small talk with the hospital staff, in preparation for another day in the OR. He was booked to give anesthesia in the *eye room*. Two pediatric strabismus cases scheduled for eye-muscle surgery, followed by three senile cataract extractions with intraocular lens implants.

When it comes to surgery, children always go in first. It is safer to keep the adults on empty stomachs for longer periods, than the youngsters. And to avoid hunger and dehydration, kids have to eat and drink as soon as possible after the operation.

Philip went in the kitchen to get some milk. He knew the topography well enough to allow safe walking in the dark. Pillow tucked under his left armpit, he opened the fridge with his right hand. Momentarily blinded by the refrigerator light, he waited for his eyes to adjust. The milk was on the second shelf. Phil grabbed it with his left hand and opened its lid with the right. He drank directly from the bottle. If Kyra saw this, he knew she would fuss. But she won't know. After putting everything back in its place, he headed for the family room, plunked down on the sofa and grabbed the TV remote.

In the family room, the automatic nightlight gave enough visibility to clearly see the buttons on the TV clicker. Newman switched the television on and scanned through, looking for something which would short-circuit his mind, change his train of thought. Something which will enable him to sleep a little. He stopped at channel 34. During a bad night, what could be more mindless than watching the good old *Happy Days*?

Ah, that Fonzie! A real sitcom hero! Always in control! Always having the last word! Always winning! A beautiful girl would like some music in Arnold's Diner? No need for money when The Fonz is around! A precise but calculated punch on the juke-box's Plexiglas and the melody starts. Another punch and total silence! But why the disappearance of colors? Why is the show now in black and white? What in the world is *Leave it to Beaver* doing on *Happy Days*?

When an exhausted anesthesiologist becomes awake enough to realize that the show he was watching on television has changed without his knowledge, he quickly makes the diagnosis that he was finally put to sleep. Why do people feel less tired when they are 100% sure they slept?

Above the television set, the clock on the TiVo box showed 5:29. Morning already! Time to get up. He shuffled quietly toward the master bathroom, stopping on his way by the bedroom just long enough to switch off the clock-radio alarm before it rang. Kyra was still peacefully asleep but, he knew well that she would soon wake up to make breakfast while he showered. Good old reliable routine. Philip felt reassured. Things should go back to normal. Things **must** go back to normal.

seven

Phil's first case was a handsome, but very unhappy, five year old blond boy named Kevin. He was used to having his beautiful blue eyes crossed. After all, his baby blues had been squinting since he was born and Kevin was happy to leave them just the way they were, no matter what mommy and daddy decided. Why change anything now? The promise of ice cream and gift toys after the operation, did not convince him to stop crying.

For Newman, this meant routine. Most children cry during the induction of anesthesia.

Strabismus surgery is a delicate procedure for the surgeon and for the anesthesiologist alike. The operation takes place only inches away from a child's airway. After all the monitoring devices are in place, the young patient is put to sleep by mask. Once asleep, and with the temporary help of a second anesthesiologist, an intravenous is started. This is followed by the insertion of an endotracheal tube, in the narrow, young windpipe. The presence or absence of loose teeth is discussed before surgery with the parents and noted on the chart.

After the intubation, the anesthesiologist observes the chest and listens to it while he inflates the lungs by squeezing the attached anesthesia bag. When satisfied that the tube is in the correct location, a protective oral airway is inserted in the mouth and the breathing pipe safely secured to the child's cheeks and jaw with adhesive tape.

Now surgery can start. The operating room table is turned in such a manner that the anesthesiologist who was at the head of the patient is now at his side. The ophthalmic surgeon, who was waiting patiently scrubbed, gowned and gloved, takes his place at the head to prepare the ocular area with antiseptic and finally start working.

The anesthesiologist is the pilot who tries to fly his patients as safely as possible through somber surgical clouds. The induction of anesthesia is the take-off, its maintenance, the flight. The emergence from anesthesia is often compared to the landing. The *arrival lounge* of the airport terminal? Where else but the recovery room?

Life in the operating room is very similar to life in a submarine: no windows, no daylight and seldom new crew members. Hours and hours of boredom interrupted by rare moments of sheer terror. Today was one of those boring days. All five ophthalmic cases went as expected. No emotions, no problems. Philip Newman MD loved being bored when working.

At quarter past four in the afternoon, Phil was in the post anesthesia care unit, talking to his last cataract patient, reassuring her that the case was indeed over and that everything went as planned. As often happens, she had problems believing it. "But only a minute ago you said to me that you're going to start!" she posed. Time flies when you're having *Milk of Amnesia.*

This patient was a tiny but sharp woman. Eighty two years old, thin, wrinkled and, judging by her curved back, probably osteoporotic. Perfect candidate for hip fractures. A typical LOL came to Philip's mind.

LOL was an old abbreviation. The flashback made Newman smile. It brought back memories of his busy internship year at the Morissania City Hospital in the Bronx, a no longer existing healthcare facility. In those days, a never ending arrival of ambulances brought people with gunshot wounds, stab wounds, heart attacks, acute abdomens and many other kinds of medical or surgical problems. Walk-in patients clogged the waiting areas. Some days there wasn't even time to use the john. When writing notes in a patient's chart, time-saving written abbreviations became second nature.

The first medical history he ever read there came to mind: *This is the 1st MCH admit of a 78 LOL INAD w/ CC of RLQ pains of 24 h. duration.* The novice intern, Newman, had no choice but approach a senior medical resident to declare his ignorance and get help with the translation: "This is the first Morissania City Hospital admission of a 78 years old Little Old Lady in no acute distress, with the chief Complaint of Right Lower Quadrant pain of twenty four hours duration." Phil often wondered whatever happened to the old medical school abbreviations in today's Internet era when CC means *Checked Contact* and LOL means *Laughing Out Loud.* Doesn't CC mean something else on television? Something like *Closed Captioning?*

A tap on the shoulder made Philip turn. It was Edward Morris, the Anesthesiology department chief, the man who mentored Phil since he was hired fresh out of residency. Ed was finishing up rounds on his recovering patients.

"Hi, Ed, how was your day?"

"Hi, Phil. Better than yours yesterday, for sure. Can I buy you a cup of coffee? We have to talk."

"Sure, Ed! Coffee shop?"

"Coffee shop it is!" The chief of anesthesia did not have his own office. Most issues were discussed in the hospital library, in the coffee shop or during get togethers in one of the anesthesiologists' homes.

"I'll meet you there. Whoever arrives first gets the table. I have to call home first. Okay, Ed?" queried Newman.

"No problem, Phil. I'm going there now. Should I order your coffee?"

Newman nodded yes. He went to the doctor's locker room to use the toilet, wash his hands and make the phone call. Cellular phones are not allowed in hospitals. Kyra was not home yet. He left a message to warn her that he might be late.

He found Dr. Morris sitting at table in the farthest corner of the hospital cafeteria, sipping his coffee. Philip sat down and started drinking his.

The chief of anesthesia was already well informed about what happened yesterday in the *plastic room,* but it was his job to learn more. He asked for details, for conceivable causes and for Phil's possible explanations. They discussed Ephedra, epinephrine allergies, and the Manhattan Eye, Ear and Throat cases.

But more importantly, Philip learned, Dr. Morris wanted to be reassured that Dr. Newman wrote everything in the chart, minute by minute, symptom by symptom, event by event. Often enough, physicians are too exhausted after a prolonged cardiac pulmonary resuscitation and opt to postpone such writing. They frequently choose to go the next day to the hospital *records room* and finish the documentation. Phil reassured him that the anesthesia record was complete.

"But if you do happen to remember something, something that you possibly forgot to write, please don't! Don't add anything to the chart."

"Why is that, Ed? What's going on?"

29

"The chart was summonsed, Phil, less than 24 hours after the event. A copy is already in the hands of an attorney. If you add something to your original record now, it will no longer match the copy in their possession and it will look like an admission of guilt. The hospital administrator spoke to me today. He has never heard of such a rapid legal action, during his entire career in the health care industry. This must be a new world record! A young man just lost his life and, his family is ready to sue and eager to collect the following day. The Walkers must have a malpractice lawyer on speed dial."

Morris took another sip of coffee and continued. "But who knows? Maybe it's just the other way around, maybe an *ambulance chaser* with insider informations contacted them and convinced them to sue. After all, today is Friday. If a law firm waits till Monday, they may lose the client to another law firm."

"Do you think I should inform my medical liability insurer?"

The chief scratched his head. "I don't think so, Phil. Not yet. Until you receive a subpoena, there's no absolute guarantee you're going to get sued. I know that our insurance company asks to be informed as early as possible. But from my own experience, I also know that if you call them now, their agents will probably call it *an event* against you and, it will automatically become a bad mark in your file. Sooner or later, you'll be penalized for doing what you're supposed to do. For complying with what they requested."

"Amazing!. Thank you for the information Ed!"

Morris looked at his watch, "Wow! Look at the time! I have to run. Are you on call this weekend?"

"I'm not."

"Have a nice weekend then, and give my regards to Kyra."

"You too, Ed!"

He called Kyra from his car, "Hi, honey. I'm finally coming home."

"Why so late?"

"Ed wanted to speak to me. He sends his regards."

"Something wrong?"

"The chart was already requested by lawyers. I'll probably get sued."

"Are you sure? I hope you're wrong Phil. Please drive safely. Supper is ready. It's Friday night and you are off this weekend off. I will open some wine..."

"No wine for me, Kyra. I'm not in the mood."

eight

Before going to bed, Phil took a shower. Why sleep in your scrub suit when you're off the next day? He put on clean pajamas and made sure the alarm clock was not on. The trouble falling asleep the night before was due to the obsession of recounting, over and over, the details of the Walker tragedy. Tonight will be a better night. Tonight **it has to be** a better night. It's true: today he was still disturbed by what happened in the operating room and by learning that he might be sued for medical malpractice, but everybody in America knows that being sued, is a fairly common occurrence, when you are an American medical doctor. He was an American doctor and, he will have no other choice but getting used to being sued. For a start, lets not allow those emotions to affect the hours of slumber. But, just to be sure, Phil took a sleeping pill at bedtime. After all, he did not have to work the next day.

Despite the sedative, Philip woke up as usual, at 5:35 in the morning. He will try to keep busy today. Being the first in the kitchen, he prepared the coffee and had scrambled eggs and toast ready, when his yawning wife arrived. Still in her nightgown, Kyra was taken aback. She could count on the fingers of one hand the number of times her husband had made breakfast.

Breakfast complete, Phil started to clear the dishes from the counter but Kyra insisted on taking over the clearing. To kill some time, he moved to the family room to watch The *Morning News* on television. But, when the clock on the *TiVo* recorder showed 8:15, Newman switched the TV off and proceeded to the garage, to start his next project: lawn mowing. Once the security system was turned off, he opened the garage door with a push of a button. It felt good to stretch a few muscle fibers on the front lawn and awaken his sleepy body, out in the fresh morning air. But what in the world was that? On the grass, just in front of him, he saw two empty cans of *Budweiser*, a one quarter full plastic bottle of *Poland Springs* and styrofoam containers from *Burger King*. Was he becoming a curmudgeon? He never felt more disgust for the people, probably teenagers, who kept the insides of their cars clean by littering other people's properties, than he felt today.

The *No Deposit No Return* concept has to go! Who invented such an idiotic idea? A five cents deposit for beer bottles and cans was not a deterrent for affluent brats, from throwing empty containers out of their car windows. What we need is a dollar. A one dollar deposit for each and every can, bottle, paper bag and food container. This would provide plenty of incentive to keep our lawns, streets, parks, lakes and rivers trash free. Homeless people will probably get together and form money making, outdoors cleaning, ecological corporations.

Philip put the beer cans in the recyclable bin and the rest of the stuff in the trash can. He was convinced that sooner or later, styrofoam would pollute the entire world. Those empty food containers and packaging peanuts were ubiquitous.

The lawnmower started without a hitch. Newman began pushing it in the regular zigzag path he found so relaxing. The clouds were dissipating as the warmth of the morning sun gradually spread. The lawnmower motor roared jarringly. Was it too early to be running his mower? The sounds coming from the lawn service company working at his neighbor's confirmed that it was not.

Newman never understood those ridiculous leaf blowers the *lawn doctors* use. After they cut your grass, they bring out those cacophonous contraptions and blow the loose stuff to the middle of the street. From there, depending on the wind, it comes back to you, or it ends up invading the neighbors' yards. The neighbors don't complain because they know their own lawn service will soon return the favor. Phil was not so gracious, and chose to share his anger on many occasions with some of the offending grass cutting guys. Waste of time.

Kyra appeared at the garage door, waving her arms. Philip turned off the mower and inquired, "Yes, Kyra?"

"Telephone. A Doctor Rooney from Los Angeles."

"Please take his number. I will call him back."

"Okay, honey."

The lawnmower restarted promptly. So did Newman. He should be done in about ten minutes. If he stopped now to answer the phone, he might not return to finish the job. He did remember a Dr. Rooney. Was it Michael Rooney? Yes, it was. Mike was a good friend of Ed Morris. He and Ed, did their residencies together at the Presbyterian Medical Center, in Manhattan. Mike was now head of the department of Anesthesiology at a Los Angeles hospital. He visited Dr. Morris at the Soundedge, last September or October. Phil remembered the three of them having coffee in the coffee shop.

The lawn was now neatly cut. The cuttings were too short to bother raking. Phil returned the mower to the garage, closed the overhead electric door and went in the house and found Kyra.

"Any coffee left?"

"Plenty."

"Great! I'll have some after I take a shower. Where did you put the phone number?"

"Next to the telephone in the den."

"Merci, mon Amour!'

She always laughed when he spoke French.

nine

"Dr. Rooney? Hi! This is Philip Newman, returning your call."

"Good morning, Dr. Newman! May I call you Phil?"

"Only if I can call you Mike!"

"Of course, Phil."

Dr. Rooney recounted how he had learned about Phil's cardiac arrest case, during his regular weekly conversation with his friend, Dr. Morris, the previous night. He wanted to share with Phil the details of a similar case at his hospital about seven months earlier.

"What do you mean by similar, Mike?"

Newman listened carefully to the explanations. The details were remarkably familiar. A young man returns from a trip abroad and is immediately brought to the hospital by his parents to have his brand new tattoos removed. The procedure was performed with Lidocaine/ epinephrine local anesthesia under Propofol sedation with the same fatal results.

Rooney continued, "Since I heard about your case, I couldn't stop thinking about it. When the first tower of the World Trade Center was hit by a plane, people were convinced that it was just a horrible accident. But when the second tower came down, everybody realized that it was no accident. As far as we know, you had the second case of cardiac arrest in a tattoo removal, of a young person, under local anesthesia, with IV sedation. You're *tower two*, Phil! Who knows? Maybe there have been more cases like this in the United States and nobody knows it!"

After a short pause to clear his voice, Rooney resumed talking. "This could be just a bizarre coincidence. But there could be something bigger afoot here. You must know that, just like the FBI doesn't talk to the CIA, hospitals don't communicate with each other. To the contrary. Hospitals are in competition for insured patients' dollars. And when it comes to interstate medical communications, the exchange of mortality information is, as far as I know, close to zero."

"How so, Mike? I can tell you have much more experience than I have on this subject."

"It's a fact, Phil. Doctors don't like to discuss their dead patients if they don't have to. You know very well that each hospital has its own private Mortality Conference and each state has its own medical liability insurance company. And even if physicians buy their malpractice coverage from an interstate company, those companies are there to sell insurance, to make money, not to play medical detective. It's easier to pay a cash settlement to the patient and raise the insurance fee for the doctor then to spend time putting two and two together."

"Were you sued on this case?"

"Of course. They asked two million dollars, but quickly settled out of court for eight hundred thousand. You know very well that if the insurance company agrees to the settlement, the physician is also forced to accept the out of court deal. If he refuses, the case goes to trial and, if the judgment is higher than the proposed settlement, the doctor has to pay the balance from his own pocket. He has no choice but to settle. As a matter of fact, both sides prefer to settle. It means less legal expenses."

"For the plaintiff, also?"

"And how. The plaintiff's lawyer spends less time on the case. He is much happier collecting his contingency fee of one third of the settlement, after writing a few papers, rather than spending days or maybe weeks in court."

"What did the autopsy show?"

"There was no autopsy. The parents refused it for religious reasons."

"Just like in my case! Tell me, Mike, when you compared my incident with *tower two,* what were you insinuating? Terrorism?"

"Of course not! I just want to say that what happened to us is probably no accident. There must be a link. A common thread. Some kind of a chemical interaction that we must investigate."

They discussed the Manhattan Eye, Ear and Throat Hospital cases, Ephedra and epinephrine. Rooney was not convinced. Hundreds of procedures are performed daily under Lidocaine/ epinephrine all around the country, with no complications. But now they'd lost two young, healthy, recently tattooed men. Why? Maybe there were some new chemicals in today's tattoo inks? Some products everyone should know about?

"Mike, you know what? You are very convincing! I will try to investigate on my side of the country. Will you make some queries on the West Coast?"

"Of course. Are you coming to the next American Society of Anesthesiologists convention? If I remember, it will take place at the Hilton in Manhattan."

"If Ed Morris gives me some time off. You probably know that he is a tough chief, don't you?"

"I will put in a good word for you."

Philip laughed, "Thank you, Mike! Then I will see you at the Hilton in about six weeks. Meanwhile, we will investigate and compare notes at the meeting. Do you use email?

"Yes. Both at home and at the hospital."

They exchanged email addresses and promises to keep in touch.

ten

Newman couldn't stop thinking about the conversation he just had with Rooney. He obsessed over the particulars while he showered, while he shaved and, when he finally got dressed. Identical events, thousands of miles apart. He had to stop thinking about those incidents. He had to put his brains on neutral. Time to take a break from the tattoo removal fixation. How about surprising Kyra by taking her out for a romantic *lupper?*

Saturday was, by far, his favorite day of the week. Particularly Saturdays during weekends off-call. After all, what comes after a Saturday off? A Sunday off! But, he knew well enough by now that Kyra hated to go out Saturday nights. Everybody went out on Saturday nights. Restaurants have waiting lists. At theaters, the *STANDING ROOM ONLY* signs rule the roost. Regular tickets are sold out. A year or so into their marriage, they reached a compromise: if they did go out on Saturday, they only ate two meals during the day: a copious late breakfast at home, and an early elegant early dinner in a good restaurant, supplanting lunch and supper. Thus the Saturday *lupper* concept was born. And the best part of *lupper* was that if you go early enough, you don't need reservations. He made plans to take her to Amelie, a gourmet French restaurant, too expensive for the *early birds* devotees.

Philip remembered they only had a modest early morning breakfast today. So what? A surprise is a surprise! It is much nicer to enjoy a good *lupper* when you're really hungry.

Should he discuss his ink tattoo theory during their romantic interlude? Should he open up to her? Will she conclude that anesthesiologists are getting paranoid across the entire country? From the Atlantic to the Pacific? From Long Island to Los Angeles? Of course, he would tell her. He had to. Kyra was the wife he always dreamed of having: a beautiful lover, a good caretaker and an intelligent counselor. First, she would probably laugh it off by using her classic teasing phrase, "I think that both of you guys are inhaling too much *laughing gas!*" But soon after that, she will start thinking about what was said and, probably come up with some advice.

They left the house just a little after one o'clock in the afternoon, to go shopping at the mall. Kyra planned this trip a week earlier. Bloomingdale's was having a *One Day Sale*. At the mall, they split up as they always did. She was going to look at dresses. He was going to look for DVDs and electronics gadgets. When she suggested meeting in the food court, he was forced to reveal the surprise. "We can meet in the food court, Kyra, but not to eat there. If you arrive there before me, please don't buy any food. We are going to Amelie for *lupper"*

The kiss she gave him was not just a wife's kiss. It was a grateful hug, mixed with the passionate embrace of a love hungry mistress. She was hopeful that her husband was recovering from his recent professional trauma.

Kyra appeared in the food court dressed in a beautiful brand new two piece suit. Darn, she looked gorgeous! Newman inquired about her purse. Nothing to worry about! It was safely tucked, together with the jeans and the T-shirt she wore this morning, in the Bloomingdale's bag she was holding in her hand. Phil reached for the paper bag and, together they started walking toward the mall parking lot.

The restaurant parking lot was pretty empty. The other advantage of *lupper* was that before 6 o'clock in the evening, parking at Amelie was self-serve. No time wasted and no money spent on pretentious valet parking. *Valet* is a French word which means butler. Why don't we call it *butler parking here* in the United States? Is it possible they call it *parking de butler* in France?

They chose a table by the window, with a view of the Amelie gardens and its graceful willows. The *sommelier* promptly presented the wine list. *Sommelier* is also a French word and it means *wine steward.* Is it possible they call him *wine steward* in Paris? Snobbism is an international disease. Like the comedian used to say: "Snobs without Borders."

Monsieur Phil will let Madame choose the wine this early evening. Tonight he was a Heineken man. At the end of the meal he will help her, if necessary, to finish the bottle. Monsieur was too cheap to leave overpriced wine in the bottle, but too shy to take it home. At least not at Amelie. Phil waited for the Chardonnay to be opened, tasted and accepted by Kyra. They ordered a *saumon sauté* for her, a *filet mignon* medium rare for him. But let's start with Caesar salads for both. Then, the obsessed anesthesiologist started recounting his newly developed theories.

The pediatric nurse listened with fascination. Amazingly enough, she did not make fun of the ink tattoo hypothesis.

"If I understand well, you are planning a visit to a tattoo parlor, Phil? To see if you can find out what's in their inks?"

"More than just visit, Kyra! I plan to experiment. I'm going to have myself tattooed in a discreet location and, a few days later, inject myself with 2 percent Lidocaine containing a one in a hundred thousand concentration of epinephrine. Don't worry sweetheart, my tattoo will have your name on it."

"Are you serious, Phil? Are you joking or are you out of your mind? If you really plan to do that, you have very little to gain and everything to lose! If you're wrong and nothing happens to you, they will end up calling you Newman the Nut at the hospital. If you're right, you will either get sick, or die! I did not marry you to become a young widow. Why don't you go on the Internet to do your research on Google rather than on your body?"

Philip was taken aback. "Wow! What a great idea Kyra, I didn't think of that! Thank you, honey! I will start tomorrow morning. In fact, why tomorrow? After all, TGIS.!" He watched her puzzled expression,. "TGIS! Don't you understand me? TGIS.! Thank God it's Saturday! Everybody knows that! If I am not too drunk when we get home, I will start my research tonight."

She laughed. Her face was illuminating when she did that.

"You know what? You look even more beautiful when you laugh Kyra."

"Flattery will get you everywhere. I begin to wonder what's behind all those compliments. Maybe you plan to experiment on me? To tattoo a deadly *'I LOVE PHILIP NEWMAN MD'* on my ass? After all, as soon as Monsieur gets rid of me, Monsieur becomes an eligible bachelor overnight.

Philip's turn to laugh. "You know what Kyra? Let's stop it. No more tattoo talk tonight! Let's discuss anything: mink, pink or sink but not a word about ink! Not a word about tattoo ink. Okay?"

"As you like it, honey. You know very well that when I drink white wine, nothing bothers me!"

They spent a very pleasant evening and it was still early when they returned home. Another advantage of *lupper*. Kyra, tipsy and sleepy, slipped into bed to watch television. Phil, impatient to get started on his research, kissed her goodnight and went to the kitchen to make coffee. He already had an *espresso* at the restaurant but his old habit of mixing *Chock full o'Nuts* with Google was too strong to resist. Coffee pot in one hand and coffee cup in the other, Philip Newman MD stepped into his den, put the pot and the cup on his desk, and booted up his computer to start his Internet quest.

After checking his email and erasing the ridiculous spam messages touting Viagra and nubile Russian brides, Phil opened Google. He decided to try typing *Tattoo Inks*. Miracle of miracles! In less than a second, he obtained the first ten results out of a possible twenty-two thousands six hundred different links for *Tattoo Inks*. He narrowed his search by adding the search word *Toxicology* after the *Tattoo Inks* phrase.

A web site named www.goaskalice.columbia.edu was answering questions on the possible adverse effects of such chemicals. Newman decided to start by opening another site. He looked over http://chemistry.about.com/library/weekly/aa121602c.htm. He read and did not believe his eyes. Mike Rooney might be on to something! Could his tattoo ink theory be right?

He started at the title: *"What Are Tattoo Inks?"* The passage explained that tattoo inks and pigments are trade secrets with uncertain contents. It went on to explain that most inks are pigments suspended in carrier solutions, primarily composed of metal salts, though sometimes plastics or vegetable dyes. The pigment supplies the tattoo color, while the suspension makes it injectable.

Phil continued to read on to the section titled *Tattoos and Toxicity*. It outlined that tattooing carried inherent toxicity and health risks. It explained that pigments and tattoo inks are not FDA regulated, but that basic information about their components could be found on their *Material Safety Data Sheets* (MSDS).

In the *Pigment Chemistry* section, one particular paragraph caught his attention. *"Allergic reactions, scarring, phototoxic reactions (i.e., reaction from exposure to light, especially sunlight), and other adverse effects are possible with many pigments. The plastic-based pigments are very intensely colored, but many people have reported reactions to them. There are also pigments that glow in the dark or in response to black (ultraviolet) light. These pigments are notoriously risky - some may be safe, but others are radioactive or otherwise toxic."*

The article continued to explain that almost anything can be used as a pigment and that many inks contain several different pigments. These different pigments carried risks and toxicities. It listed a long array of pigments and their likely chemical contents. It mentioned black, brown, red, orange, flesh, yellow, green, blue, violet and white. The most dangerous appeared to be the red color. It included chemicals like Cinnabar (HgS), Cadmium Red (CdSe), Iron Oxide (Fe2O3), and Napthol-AS pigment.

Phil found the passage on red pigments even more alarming. *"Iron oxide is also known as common rust. Cinnabar and cadmium pigments are highly toxic. Napthol reds are synthesized from Naptha. Fewer reactions have been reported with naphthol red than the other pigments, but all reds carry risks of allergic or other reactions."*

Newman realized that he had absolutely no idea what the colors on James Walker's tattoos were. Nobody ever dreamed having to write down the tattoo colors in a patient's charts. Most often the chart doesn't even note if a person is bearded or clean shaven, never mind the color of his tattoos. He decided to send the link to the article by email to Dr. Rooney. In his letter, Newman asked if the Los Angeles patient had a red tattoo. And just to be funny, Philip added, "The Long Island one also had long hair and a big beard. How about yours?"

Phil returned to reading the article. He became both engrossed and horrified to learn about the lack of controls and regulations of liquids used as carriers for tattoo inks. It discussed some safe liquids commonly used, but then proceeded with much more alarming information. *"However, many other substances have been and may be used, including: denatured alcohols (are toxic and can burn the skin) other alcohols (methyl alcohol or methanol and isopropyl alcohol or rubbing* alcohol are commonly used, although they are toxic) ethylene glycol (antifreeze, which is toxic) aldehydes, such as formaldehyde and gluteraldehyde (highly toxic) various surfactants or detergents."

By now, Phil Newman was completely engrossed. Wasn't *Ethylene Glycol* the stuff they found in recalled Chinese toothpaste? He continued to read: *"There are many other substances that could be found in an ink. A tattooist has the choice of mixing his or her own ink (mixing dry dispersed pigment and a carrier solution) or purchasing what are called pre-dispersed pigments. Many pre-dispersed pigments are as safe as or safer than inks mixed by the tattooist. However, the ingredient list need not be disclosed, so any chemical could be present in the ink. The best advice is to make sure the ink supplier and the particular ink has a long history of safety. Although I have applied the word 'toxic' to many substances listed on the pigment and carrier list, that is an oversimplification. Some of these chemicals are mutagens, carcinogens, dermatogens, toxins, or participate in other reactions in the body, some of which may not show up for decades."*

The article concluded with more startling caveats, *"Even if you have quality pigments and use the recommended carriers to mix the ink, there are other, less obvious potential health hazards associated with tattoo inks: alcohol makes skin more permeable. This means that when alcohol is used in the ink or to disinfect the skin's surface, it allows more chemicals to cross into the bloodstream than ordinarily would."*

"Another interesting factoid concerning alcohol is that it is known as a 'promoter.' In biomedical parlance, this means alcohol works synergistically with mutagens, teratogens, and carcinogens to make them more likely to cause harm than they would by themselves. If any hazardous substances are present in the ink, alcohol helps them into the body and then increases the chance that they may cause mutation or disease, not just at the site of the tattoo, but throughout the body."

"Medical-grade chemicals are intended for medical uses, so any impurities within them should be relatively safe. However, the trace amounts of contaminants in high purity chemicals from a chemical supply house may be extremely toxic substances! An example: distilled water that isn't intended for drinking, while technically pure, can have highly toxic organic chemicals as contaminants."

"The person who mixes the ink needs to understand proper sterilization techniques. This includes knowing how to perform heat-sterilization and cold-sterilization and understanding the sterilization needs of different materials. Dry or mixed pigments should never be heat sterilized, since the heat can cause chemical changes in the pigment molecules, sometimes producing toxic substances."

Philip realized that there was absolutely no point in visiting a tattoo parlor. If tattooists are allowed to mix their own inks, how could anybody learn what went wrong? How could you compare? And if the health authorities are as lax as they are in the United States, imagine how lax they are overseas? Rooney's patient was tattooed abroad. Newman suddenly realized that he had absolutely no idea in what country had James Walker gotten tattooed. He never thought to ask.

Before he switched off the computer, Phil checked one last time his email. Old habit. The answer from Los Angeles was already there. "Thank you for the information, Phil. I have no idea what color the tattoo was, but...guess what? Our patient was also bearded and had long hair. Speak to you soon. Mike."

eleven

After his intense Google session, and despite all the beer and wine he had drank at Amelie's, Philip felt totally revived. Life is often unexplainably bizarre. When he sat in front of a television screen, he frequently fell asleep sitting on the sofa. But in front of the computer screen, he always felt awake and energized. Probably just the basic difference between a passive and an active involvement. After a quick wash, Phil brushed his teeth and finally went to bed. Not because he was tired. Not because he wanted to sleep. He went to bed because it was getting late. He went to bed because it was time to go to bed.

In the bedroom, his better half was already asleep with the television blasting. He lowered the volume, changed the station and put the TV timer on, hoping to find himself, by the time the television turned itself off, in the arms of Morpheus. He did.

The next day, during breakfast, Kyra told Philip that she had plans to play tennis with girlfriends that morning. He was delighted to hear that. A little Sunday morning solitude was heaven. *The New York Times* was waiting in the driveway to be read, professional problems were waiting in his head to be solved and he also had a phone call to make. Phil liked to chat now and then, at length, with the retired ex-head of the Soundedge Anesthesiology department, Dr. Arthur Ross. He loved his sense of humor.

Newman read the Sunday newspaper until 10 o'clock. He poured through section after section for any follow-ups on the Manhattan Eye, Ear and Throat Hospital story to no avail. Exactly at 10, he put down the paper and called his ex-chief. It was Dr. Ross himself who answered.

"Good Morning, Arthur! Phil Newman calling."

"Good morning! How are you, my young man?" The 76 year old physician called all his still practicing colleagues "young men."

"Surviving in this cruel world."

"Yes, I know. I heard about your case, Phil."

"I thought you were retired, Arthur!"

"I'm retired, but not dead. I do keep up with international, national and local events."

"Art, I think I'm going to get sued."

"Welcome to the group! Show me a busy practicing anesthesiologist in this country who claims he was never sued and I'll show you a liar."

"So you were sued?"

"Are you kidding me? Are you checking to see if I'm a liar? Of course I was sued! Today I'm the happiest man in the world. I finally got over my two biggest fears in life."

"Dr. Arthur Ross, fearful? I don't believe it. And what exactly were you afraid of?"

"Number one, afraid of dying young and, number two, afraid of being sued for medical malpractice after I retire. Now it is, thank God, too late for both."

"How can you be so sure?"

"No longer being able to die young, it's obvious I think. You must know my age by now, dear Dr. Newman. You see? I'm in a much better position than you are, my friend. You could still die young. Not me. And I can no longer be sued because the statute of limitations have expired."

"What's that, Art? It's new to me. I was never sued before."

"A doctor who has never heard of statutes of limitations! You must be living a protected life, Philip Newman. The statute of limitations is the legal term. It says that a physician can be sued for a period of thirty months after an event. Therefore, if an incident took place during your last working day, it will take 30 months after your retirement, before you could stop being afraid of opening the door to strangers. Particularly, anyone appearing to carry legal papers."

"And what exactly did you do to avoid being sued after retirement, Arthur?

"Prevention, Phil, prevention! During the two and a half years before retirement, I was forced to practice the ugly and unethical, but preventive art: *defensive medicine.*"

"You mean staying away from difficult cases and avoiding helping colleagues in trouble?"

"You hit the nail on the head! Each and every time your name ends up on a medical chart, you run the risk of ending up in court. Even if you were helping a colleague in distress. When it comes to hospital based physicians, there is no such a thing as a Good Samaritan Law. Lawyers love Good Samaritans carrying medical liability insurance."

"And what did you do if nobody else was available to give anesthesia to a risky case?"

"I found reasons to cancel or postpone the operation, until one of the young guys was free. You know the system: repeat the fasting blood sugar test, ask for more units of blood on stand-by, etc. And in the cases I was actually involved, I used the old CYA method."

"CYA? Cover your ass?"

"Yes sir, cover my ass! I ordered every possible preop lab work in the book. Lawyers make you look bad in court when they ask for the results of a test which you haven't ordered. You tell the jury 'unnecessary test,' they tell the jury 'negligent medical care.' In our days, everybody has to cover their asses. Just like the baby carriage manufacturer who puts a warning label on each stroller saying *REMOVE CHILD BEFORE FOLDING*."

"We live in a sad world, Arthur. It this why we went through medical school, internship and three years of Anesthesiology residency?"

"C'est la vie, Philip. Adapt to it!"

"Being sued for malpractice must be a very depressing experience. I think that if this ends up happening to me, I will quit anesthesia."

"And what exactly are you going to do? Stay home and let your wife work for both of you? Become a gigolo? We all went through that, my friend. I even looked for another job once."

"Did you find anything?"

"It's not easy to find a position when you're as ultra-specialized as we are. Please don't take me too seriously Phil, but, for a while, I thought of applying for an opening at the State Capital in Albany."

"To do what?"

"To become an executioner!"

"An executioner?"

"Yes, an executioner is an obvious job for an anesthesiologist, Philip. Today, the electric chair is obsolete. People are sent to the eternal sleep with an intravenous infusion in which an overdose of medications is injected. Who is more qualified than us? All we would have to get used to is the tripling of the usual drug doses. In the end, I decided not apply because I was not able to obtain the answer to an important question."

"And the important question was?"

"What happens if the customer survives? Can I be sued? Do I have to buy *executioner malpractice insurance*?"

Newman couldn't stop laughing. "You're a riot, Dr. Ross! And instead of killing people you decided to continue trying to save lives!"

"In a defensive way. Take care of one easy case after another."

"Of course it was easy for you to select your cases; You were the chief of the group. You made the decisions about who does what. Hail to the chief!"

"You hit the nail on the head again, Phil! Just make sure that you also become the chief of anesthesia before the end of your career and everything will be all right."

"You never stop making me laugh, Arthur! I always know I can count on your good advice."

"Any time, Dr. Newman! Give my love to Mrs. Newman."

"Only if you give my love to Mrs. Ross."

"With pleasure. But I will be able to do that, only if she decides to talk to me tonight. By tomorrow, I will probably forget!"

"Tell her that I insist she be nice to you. You're my hero!"

"I will tell her what you just said, for sure! Have a nice Sunday."

twelve

Like most early Sunday mornings, Doctor Maloney was, weather permitting, on the golf course. Today was no different. He finished playing minutes past 11:00. The black Cadillac's trunk, opened by remote control, was patiently awaiting the arrival of his bag. But the surgeon kept on chatting with a golf cart pushing friend about birdies and pars until a beeping sound came from inside the car. "Fred, I have to leave you now. I have messages. Have a nice day."

"You too, Jesse," Fred replied.

With the golfing equipment now safely locked inside the luggage compartment, Maloney entered the car and pushed around the papers lying on the passenger front seat, until he found the buried cell phone. His answering service wanted a callback. He removed the cell phone attached to the belt of his pants and pressed the speed dial.

"Maloney speaking."

"Dr. Maloney. Margaret Kane, the Soundedge OR supervisor, would like to talk to you. She's at home." He jotted the number on a piece of paper.

"Thanks! Have a nice day and let's keep it quiet."

"We'll try."

Margaret answered on the first ring.

"Peggy? Jesse here. I'm returning your call."

"Good morning, Jesse. How come I have to leave messages? You don't believe in carrying your cell phone with you?"

"I prefer to call back when I can and when I feel like it, Peg, not when I'm being interrupted. My answering service decides if it's urgent and necessary to have somebody from the club find me on the golf course, rather than leave messages. You know well that Port Lincoln voted against building a cell-phone tower. Not only the reception is sporadic around here but how many daily emergencies do cosmetic surgeons have? Urgent liposuctions?"

"Are we in a funny mood this morning, or what?"

"It happens once in a while. And what can I do for you, my favorite nurse?"

"I would like to talk to you over lunch. I'm buying."

"I'm at my country club. Only members can buy here. But you're invited! Do you know how to get here?"

"Of course, my favorite plastic surgeon! I've had lunch at your club a couple of times. You even took me there for supper once. How quickly men forget!"

Was she sure that he was the one who took her here? He was not going to be a wiseass and ask. What was the point? After all, it was probably true and, if it was true, it must have happened soon after his divorce. When Nancy left him for a younger man, he became temporarily insane. The year of his breakup was a total blur in his memory. All he remembered was doing everything possible, to avoid being alone. "You know what, Peg? I'm going to shower now. I'll see you in the dining room in 45 minutes. Enough time for you?"

"Okay, Jesse. I'll be there at 12.30."

Maloney looked at his watch. "12.30? Perfect! Bye for now."

"Bye. See you soon."

His gray hair was still shower-wet when the Maitre D' sat him down at his favorite table by the window, with a panoramic view of the Long Island Sound. On clear days, like today, you could see the Connecticut coast across the water as a free bonus.

Jesse was wondering why Margaret Kane wanted to see him. A little face lift maybe? Just the eyelids? Botox? Of all the operating room nurses, Peggy was the most disadvantaged when wearing the surgical garb. The difference between Peggy in scrubs and Peggy in a low-cut evening dress, with a trace of décolleté and with her beautiful reddish hair flowing freely, was enormous. A night and day difference.

"Here you are, Dr. Maloney!"

He stood up to shake her hand but, she kissed him on both cheeks. "You look great, Peg. I hope you're not planning cosmetic surgery!"

"Are you going to like me better if I get some?" She sat on the chair across, facing the surgeon and looking directly into his brown eyes.

Maloney sat down, too. "Are you flirting with me, Peg?"

"Just a little, Jesse. Don't forget that this tough operating room supervisor is also a woman." Looking through the window, Margaret waved her right hand. Following her eyes, Maloney waved, too. Jennifer

Davis and Kyra Newman were passing by smiling and waving at them with their tennis rackets.

Peggy continued. "I didn't come here to talk about me. I came to speak to you about the Walker case."

thirteen

The familiar noise of the electric garage door opener, startled Newman. His wife was back from playing tennis. Kyra popped her head in the door. "I'm back, honey! Are you decent? I brought a friend. I invited Jennifer for a cup of coffee."

Jennifer Davis was a good friend of Kyra's and a great tennis player. An ex-hospital RN who left a supervising nursing position at Soundedge, to work with her urologist husband William Davis.

"I'm still in my pajamas. Is that decent enough for a Sunday morning?"

"Decent enough for me," shouted Jennifer from the garage. "Believe me, Phil, I've seen much worse in Bill's office." Kyra allowed her friend to step in the house first. She followed just behind.

"Good morning, Dr. Newman."

"Good afternoon, Mrs. Davis. Time flies when you're playing tennis! How do you keep yourself so young and beautiful? What's your secret?"

"I'm not young and beautiful. Just well preserved. Bill keeps me in formaldehyde."

"Very funny! How was tennis?"

"We played doubles and lost. But it was a good game."

"My better half behaved?"

"She always does, when she's with me."

"Is this true, Kyra?"

"If Jenny says so, it must be true."

Both ladies put their tennis racquets on the floor, against the wall. Kyra started making the coffee. "Two cups or three? Are you going to join us, Phil?"

"Only if you insist."

"I insist. My friend here has some news for you."

"Good news, I hope. I can't wait."

"After they took their first sips, Jennifer said, "Bill told me about James Walker."

"Those Soundedge people have a big mouth."

"Not exactly, Phil. James was my husband's patient. You didn't know that?"

"Walker needed an urologist? He was only nineteen years old with no medical history."

"No medical history? Are we talking about the same person? Bearded with long hair? Didn't he look very much like that other Walker....what was his name? John Walker? You know who I'm talking about. The young American man discovered in Afghanistan among the Taliban? You must have seen him. He was shown many times on television."

"Wow! You're right Jen! He looked exactly like him. Wow! When I saw James Walker, I knew he reminded me of somebody but I couldn't put my finger on it."

"That seeming healthy young man had cancer, Philip. A very bad cancer! Bill diagnosed malignant testicular choriocarcinoma when he was seventeen and removed one of his testicles. That's all they would agree to. No laparotomy, no abdominal exploration to clean out any involved nodes, no nothing. Quite a narcissistic young man. Like I said, he was only seventeen at the time but, it didn't stop him from refusing chemotherapy. He didn't want to lose his hair. And believe it or not, the father went along with his son's wishes."

"They gave away the only chance for a cure!"

"Exactly! I was forced to make them sign a legal release form. Your operating room supervisor...what's her name...Margaret Kane was present and she was kind enough to help me explain to them why signing is necessary in cases of treatment refusal. Peggy signed the form, too, as a witness. I remember it like it was yesterday. Maybe vanity kept Walker from disclosing the missing testicle when you admitted him."

"Peggy? Peggy Kane? What in the world was she doing there?"

"As far as I know, Peg was his father's companion. They came to the office together. The man is a widower. She probably is still his girlfriend."

"I'm going to stop by the hospital records room to look at his previous chart. I'm dying to read the operative report."

"The operation wasn't done at your hospital. Bill gave them the choice between Soundedge and the St. Joseph Hospital in Ferrytown. He's on the surgical staff at both locations. I was really surprised when your own operating room supervisor advised them to go to the other hospital. Maybe she didn't want the pressure of having him as a patient. After all, St. Joseph's is only fifteen miles away, on the South Shore."

"What a pity! I would love to read the report."

"You know what? Stop by our office tomorrow. We have copies of everything. I will tell Bill you're coming and, even if he can't be there, I will be. I have paper work to do."

"Thank you, Jen. I don't know my schedule yet but, as soon as I'm done, I'll come over. Do you guys make good coffee?"

"An espresso machine is good enough for you?."

"Mmmm.... I love espresso! In that case, I won't bother stopping by the hospital coffee shop after work. See you tomorrow. I'm now going to take a shower, shave and get dressed."

"Bye, Phil! I will probably not be here when you return. Will you come with Phil tomorrow, Kyra?"

"My shift ends at four o'clock. It all depends at what time Phil gets done."

"See you tomorrow, guys, one or both of you. And by the way, Phil, did you know that Peggy Kane is having lunch with Jesse Maloney as we speak?"

fourteen

For Philip Newman, the Monday schedule was repetitive, but easy. Three laparoscopic cholecystectomies, each usually lasting about ninety minutes. But if you included the cleaning and the sterilization of the OR between each case, the time span was more like two hours. Phil was convinced that the laparoscopic approach was probably one of the most important of all recent advances in surgery. The patient goes home the next day with a few tiny holes in his or her belly, and minus the sick gallbladder. He could not forget the olden times when his poor mother spent eight excruciating days in the hospital, after recovering from the side to side abdominal incision, necessary at the time, to remove this organ. The operation was semi-urgent. Her gallbladder was totally filled with stones.

If there were no emergencies added to his caseload today, he should be done by two o'clock in the afternoon. At that hour, Kyra would still be working. He'd go to Dr. Davis's office alone. It was better that way, anyway.

He had to go there today. It was a must. Tomorrow was Tuesday and on Tuesday he was scheduled to be *on-call*. Despite the cell phone attached to his belt, Philip did not travel outside the area when *on-call*. He liked to be nearby and accessible at all times. Old fashioned Newman was not able to adapt to modern gadgets. He felt that when an anesthesiologist is *on-call*, he has to be present either at home or at the hospital. Not in restaurants, Little League games or Barnes and Noble. Not to gallivant around like the younger doctors do in our days. After all, cell phones are not always reliable.

He finished work at exactly 1:30. Anxious to see James Walker's operative record, Phil didn't bother going home to change. Jennifer and Bill would not mind seeing him in his hospital garb. After all, she saw him at home yesterday in his pajamas. No difference between the two. As soon as he was in his car, he used his cell phone to call the urologist.

Jennifer answered, "Doctor Davis's office. May I help you?"

"I sure hope you can. My urinary flow is perfect but I heard that your cappuccino is better than the brew at Starbucks. Is this true?"

"This must be Dr. Philip Newman, the famous gaspasser and coffee connoisseur! Are you coming, Phil? The chart is waiting on my desk and the espresso machine is ready. Like I said yesterday, all I have to do is push the button."

"How in the world did you know that anesthesiologists call each other 'gaspassers?' I thought that this was our professional secret. A secret password between gaspassers! But I forgot that nurse Davis knows everything. I'm leaving Soundedge now, Jenny. I should be there in about five minutes See you soon."

"Okay Phil."

Dr. William Davis's car was not outside his office. He was probably still operating. In the waiting room, a couple of patients were seated, quietly reading weekly publications. They didn't even lift their eyes from their magazines when Philip entered, surgically clad. Jennifer was on the phone. Pointing to the chart, she signaled Phil to step in.

Newman stood next to the desk and picked up James Walker's chart. After sitting during three gall bladder surgeries and driving the car, it felt good to stand up. At the end of her phone conversation, the efficient nurse kissed him quietly on the cheek and left him alone in the office, closing the door behind. Time to reassure her waiting patients that the doctor had just called and was on his way in from the South Shore.

The diagnosis on the chart was exactly what was explained the day before: *TESTICULAR CHORIOCARCINOMA*. Margaret Kane, RN, was the co-signer of the *Refusal of chemotherapy and/or of possible follow-up surgery* form. Dangerous diagnosis, disastrous prognosis when left untreated. Jenny did not forget a thing. Everything she mentioned was there. Even the fact that the patient and his father chose the St. Joseph Hospital on Peggy's advice, was written down.

Philip decided not to wait for the espresso. He was eager to go home. When you face the possibility of working non-stop for over 24 hours the next day, being home today, is paradise! He thanked Jennifer, sent his regards to Bill, said goodbye to the waiting patients, and left.

But first, he went back to the hospital to see his post-op patients. The first two ladies were already in their rooms, sitting up in their beds and chatting with visitors. The third one, a man, was still in the recovery room but ready to go upstairs. All three were relieved and pleased that surgery was over.

Kyra was not home at his arrival. He prepared his own strong coffee, put some music on and comfortably sat on the sofa in the den, sipping his steamy drink. Philip desperately wanted to relax, in spite of the fact that he could clearly feel the obsessive behavior making a strong comeback. Once again Phil couldn't stop thinking about the events. He analyzed the situation non stop..

Was it a possible common link between the Manhattan, the Los Angeles and the Port Lincoln OR fatalities? Did they all involve Ephedra and epinephrine followed by a fatal allergic reaction? How about the possible tattoo inks link between Mike Rooney's case and James Walker? Had the toxic effects of the tattoo inks interacted with the anesthetics? Was there something more sinister going on? Could Walker, the man who opted to refuse lifesaving treatment for cancer, deliberately withhold his medical history because he wanted to die in the O.R.? After all, if he died on the operating room table, his family could make money from a malpractice settlement. If he simply died from his cancer, they would make nothing. This could be a very lucrative form of suicide for a desperate young man facing a certain demise.

Such plot could only have been designed by his hateful, vengeful ex-mistress, Peggy Kane. She was the one who sent the patient to the St. Joseph Hospital. It was surely her idea that it was better for the testicular choriocarcinoma diagnosis not to be written down in James Walker's Soundedge chart. And who else but her, would know that if they allowed the autopsy to take place, the para-aortic and any other metastatic spread of the cancer would surely be discovered? Only she would know that a next-of-kin who refuses the post-mortem examination, has the legal right to invoke religious reasons, without having the obligation to show proof. Philip Newman MD sued for medical malpractice? This was a real sweet revenge for Peggy Kane.

And what about the surgeon? How about Jesse Maloney? He seemed a bit nonchalant during the resuscitations attempts. Unconcerned. Why was he having lunch with Peggy yesterday? What was going on? A conspiracy? Was he the victim of a conspiracy?

Philip Newman suddenly became cognizant that this was no longer a case of being obsessive. He was becoming neurotic and paranoid. The belief that the entire world was now against him, was taking root. A world full of adversity. An enemy in every corner. He was going crazy!

He had to stop! After all, there was no way for Margaret Kane to have known in advance that he would be the one to administer the anesthesia for the tattoo removal, There was no special request for Dr. Newman on the OR schedule the day of the operation. The *plastic room* was assigned to him the night before, in the usual manner, by Ed Morris.

Why would Jesse Maloney be involved? After all, if Newman gets sued, Maloney gets sued. The chart has only been subpoenaed. Maybe they won't get sued. Enough with such nonsense!

Engrossed in his thoughts, Phil did not even hear the garage door open. Kyra was already in the living room when he heard the familiar "Anybody home?" Phil got up and welcomed his wife with a kiss.

fifteen

It was another beautiful sunny Monday morning in Los Angeles. At Mount David Hospital, the surgical schedule was unusually light. Once in a while it does happen that a few patients choose not to have their elective surgery done at the beginning of the week. But more often than not, the culprits are the surgeons and their love for an occasional prolonged weekend. When two surgeons decide to extend their weekends at the same time, the result is a quiet Monday.

This unexpected hiatus suited Dr. Michael Rooney perfectly. The chief of the Anesthesiology department had things to do, articles to read, letters to write. After helping several cases start on time and assisting with the difficult intubation of a 480 pound patient about to undergo gastric stapling, Mike let everybody know where he could be found, if needed: in the medical library by the internet computer.

He didn't have to stop by the cafeteria for a pick-me-up either. The library had its own coffee supplies and a caring 62 year old librarian, Mrs. Ramón, who always made sure the coffee was fresh. But Rooney hated drinking from a paper cup. He always brought his own *Diprivan* coffee cup, an advertising gift from a drug company.

Dr. Rooney was determined to continue investigating his tattoo inks suspicions. The internet links sent to him from Long Island reinforced his beliefs. He composed an explanative letter asking for information from any concerned anesthesiologists, and decided to publish his request by email on the web page of the American Society of Anesthesiologists and to also send copies to colleagues he personally knew.

"TO WHOM IT MAY CONCERN:

During the last year, I was made aware of two unexpected and unexplained cardiac arrests occurring during removal of tattoos under local anesthesia supplemented by intravenous sedation. With the hope of solving the mystery and in search of common links, I would like to hear from every anesthesiologist involved in the past 5 years in similar cases. It doesn't matter if the tattoos were removed by laser, dermabrasion or surgical excision, as long as intravenous sedation or general anesthesia was necessary.

Please send me as much information as possible: age, sex, race, medical history, medications taken at home (and especially antidepressants), allergies, facial and other anatomical features of patients, the possibility of anabolic steroids abuse, the color of the tattoo inks involved (if available), amounts and concentrations of anesthetics, duration of the procedure, complications (if any) and, if fatal outcomes, the autopsy findings and legal consequences.

Let's get together and make the practice of Anesthesiology as safe as humanly possible Please send all the data to my email address.

Thank you. Michael Rooney MD, DA"

The emphasis on antidepressants was caused by the recent drug manufacturers' revelations of increased suicidal risk in children and adolescents taking any of the more of the 3 dozens tranquilizers on the market. But he knew that the chances for such suicides to occur while under anesthesia were, for sure, minimal. The risks attached to anabolic steroids intake came to mind because of non-stop media reports of deadly results in young abusers. There were no concrete studies on a connection between anabolic steroids and anesthesia complications, but the formation of thrombi after steroids usage was a known fact. Those blood clots could easily circulate and kill a patient during the vaso-dilatation period caused by anesthetics.

Keeping up with daily medical news and with all the televised *Ask your Doctor* pharmaceutical commercials kept Michael Rooney puzzled. How could we have dozens of medications on the market competing to protect us from depression, a handful of drugs ready to prevent stomach acid and three well advertised pills against erectile dysfunction, but, winter after winter after winter, not enough vaccine to forefend the flu?

sixteen

Being on-call, was no longer what it used to be. In the beginning of his medical career, a 3:00 in the morning telephone call made Newman feel important. It made him feel needed. It made him jump out of bed, ready to save the world.

Now, too many years later, Philip wished he felt less needed and more rested. Athletes don't retain Olympic form forever. Why are physicians expected to retain everlasting energies?

Anesthesiologists on call never go home for lunch and almost never for supper. They are scheduled to keep patients alive and pain free during surgery, in the *long room*. The *long room* is the operating room which will probably finish the latest in the day. The time spent in the OR is followed by post-operative rounds on their own surgical convalescents and preoperative rounds on next day's inpatients. Informative telephone calls have to be made to colleagues on the kind of cases and medical problems they will face, in their respective OR's, the day after.

By the time the elective surgery, medical rounds and phone calls are finished, emergencies are piled up. When on call, Newman usually went home between 11 PM and 3 AM No telephone calls after 3 AM was labeled a *good call*. This was rare. Very rare. Most anesthesia calls were *bad calls*.

The following day, if nobody in the anesthesia group was sick or away on vacation, Newman had a day off. Otherwise he was scheduled to perform in the *short room*. And being the first to finish working, often meant being the only one available, when a surgical patient in acute distress arrives by ambulance and all the other OR's are busy.

Philip finished the elective surgery cases at 5 PM and medical rounds at 7 PM. The first doctor he called was Edward Morris, his anesthesia chief, who gave him a rundown of the group's schedule for the next day. At the end of their conversation, Morris asked: "Do you have time to chat a little, Philip?"

"Not really, Ed. After I speak to the guys about tomorrow, I have an appendectomy which will probably be bumped by an abdominal exploration. Also there is a possible ruptured spleen in the ER. An MVA"

"No problem, Phil. You're off tomorrow. Give me a call when you can."

"I will, Ed. Have a good night."

Newman went to bed at 4:15 in the morning.

seventeen

"Happiness is..." Since prehistoric times, humans have been trying to define the impossible; *What is Happiness?* The answers are multiple and, more often than not, they depend on who is asking the question. It all hinges on age, sex, health, profession or on the amount of money in one's bank account. Tonight for Philip Newman, just like for the majority of anesthesiologists on-call, the answer was simple; happiness is when the phone doesn't ring after you go to bed. Going to sleep totally exhausted past 4 o'clock in the morning with the expectation of jolting telephonic sounds brings total jubilation when you open your eyes the next day, the sun is shining and nothing has happened. On days off, Phil's alarm clock was off, too. When he finally woke up, Newman looked at the clock and did not believe his eyes; 10:45 in the morning! He had slept over six hours non-stop, without dreams or interruptions. He didn't even hear when his wife left for work. This was happiness. Real happiness! The *bad call* ended up not so bad after all.

His breakfast was waiting on the kitchen counter with a short sweet note from Kyra at its side. The electric percolator was ready. *Chock Full o'Nuts* coffee in the filter and water above. The almost full can of coffee was left on the counter next to the coffee maker, just in case her husband wanted to make some more "pick-me-up" drinks later. Phil did not recognize the coffee can. The name was the same but the packaging seemed new. He took it in his hand to examine it all around. Aha! The Sara Lee company has finally removed the image of the Twin Towers from their *Heavenly Coffee*'s label. About time!

It took the push of one finger to turn the machine on. Now all Philip had to do was take the milk out of the refrigerator, pour it on the bowl of cereal and wait for the coffee to slowly drip. But why wait? Enough time was wasted by his late sleep. If he showered and shaved now, the coffee would be ready and waiting by the time he's done.

Newman did not plan to go to the hospital today. Yesterday's minor surgery patients had gone home by now, for sure. The other ones, the ones who underwent major operations like the appendectomy and the splenectomy, would still be in their beds tomorrow. He decided to remain at home, catch up on his emails and make some phone calls. First he had to call his chief. But Philip Newman felt awake enough to call Ed Morris, only after finishing his second cup of the black brew.

"Good morning, Ed."

"Hi Phil. Your splenectomy was just leaving the recovery room when I arrived this morning. He was going to the intensive care unit for observation. He seemed awake and stable."

"Thanks. He did well last night. He needed only two pints of blood. I will see him first thing in the morning tomorrow, before the schedule starts. What did you want to talk to me about?"

"Mike Rooney. I know he called you. Did you get his email? He talks about two mortality cases, both tattoo removals. Is one of the two yours?"

"For sure. It has to be. We talked at length about such cases. I haven't checked my email yet. What exactly is he saying?"

"He would like to hear from every anesthesiologist around the country who was involved in similar procedures to compare notes and search for common links. I think that using the Internet to investigate unexpected occurrences in different hospitals is a fantastic idea! If health care facilities communicated with each other, some of Charles Cullen's victims will still be alive today."

"Charles Cullen? Who are you talking about?"

"The male nurse arrested in December 2003 at the Somerset Hospital in New Jersey, after murdering a priest with an overdose of intravenous digoxin. Don't you remember the story? Once the investigation started, they found out that the man had killed between 30 and 40 patients in different hospitals in Pennsylvania and New Jersey. For sixteen years! From about 1987 to 2003. Some hospitals were suspicious but did nothing about it, some hospitals just let him go and the others he left on his own. But the number of registered complaints against this animal was zero. The Nursing Board file on Charles Cullen was empty in both states. Either from ignorance, stupidity or a total code of silence."

"It's coming back to me. I must have seen it on *48 Hours* or *60 Minutes*, I'm not sure on which one. If I remember correctly, they nicknamed the guy something like *The Angel of Death*"

"Exactly! The story came to my mind after I became informed about the Los Angeles OR death, which took place about eight months ago. Maybe it's our turn to learn from the Charles Cullen's case."

"What do you mean by that? To learn what?"

"Do we really know where any of the staff who came to work in our operating room in the past eight months came from? Doctors or nurses? Do we know if anybody worked in the Mount David Hospital operating room during their tattoo removal with cardiac arrest case?"

"You're becoming paranoid Ed. Just like me. But to tell you the truth, I didn't think about such a possibility. What you say makes sense. Lots of sense. Doctor Rooney has his own suspicions, and I have mine. And now, you bring a totally new angle to our investigation. It shouldn't be too difficult to exchange lists of people working in our surgical suites and compare. Do you also want to compare lists of our OR personnel with the Manhattan Eye, Ear and Throat Hospital?"

"Why not. Maybe a crazy person replaced their *One in a Hundred Thousand* epinephrine solution with a more concentrated vaso-constrictor or maybe even with something else. Something toxic, poisonous. Who knows? There must be more than one Charles Cullen in the world. Theoretically, each and every hospital could have one or more of those maniacs. But I do know that the Manhattanites are doing their own in-depth investigation. They don't need us. I will just ask Margaret Kane to get in touch with Rooney's OR supervisor."

"Margaret Kane? Why get her involved? Please Ed, don't get Peggy mixed in this. We are talking about death under anesthesia. Let us investigate. The fewer people we make aware of our suspicions, the fewer the potential leaks and the better our chances of solving this mystery. Sherlock Holmes follows his leads on his own. He never delegates."

"I see you still don't trust your ex-girlfriend, Phil. But you're maybe right. I see your point. I will take care of it."

"It will be very interesting to see if Mike gets any positive replies from all those emails."

"This is why I wanted to speak to you. To make sure that he knows all about our case."

"Believe me, he does."

"By the way, what do you know about the previous hospital appointments of Bob Raye, the surgical male nurse?"

"All I know is that he was once a medic in Vietnam."

"That's all you know?"

It followed a moment of silence, Newman scratched his head with his free hand. "That's all I know, chief."

"Okay Phil. We'll take it from here. Enjoy your day off.."

"Thanks, Ed." He put down the telephone receiver.

The next morning, Newman left home earlier than usual. On the operating room schedule, he was in charge with providing the anesthesia for gynecological procedures: 3 dilatation & curettage, 2 tubal ligations and one laparoscopy (possible laparotomy) for ovarian cyst. All morning admissions.

But Phil decided to first fill up the almost empty gas tank in his car before going to the hospital to start post-op rounds. The good doctor had already made sure that the appendectomy and the splenectomy patients from two nights ago, were still in their beds. It was a department of anesthesia procedure to double check on the phone with the nurses in charge, before going up to visit the surgical floors. It is a very common occurrence for patients to sign themselves out of the hospital without physician's consent. Anesthesiologists don't like to examine the wrong patient lying sedated in the right bed or, even worse, waste precious time before, during or after the OR cases, only to be faced with empty bunks.

On his arrival at the round-the-clock self-service gas station, Phil couldn't believe his eyes: Jesse Maloney was pulling out in a black monstrosity -a brand new H2. The plastic surgeon who had proclaimed how he hated Hummers, the man who repeatedly professed his disgust for gas guzzlers, was now driving one. Ludicrous!

Philip knew most surgeons' opinions by heart. After all, he had no choice but listen to them over and over again. The more routine and the longer a surgical procedure was, the wider the exchange of thoughts. The conversations taking place in the course of prolonged cosmetic operations were probably the most comprehensive. During never ending facelifts and eternal tummy-tucks, the doctors often discussed solutions to the world's problems: crooked attorneys, medical, national or international politics, economy, insurance prices, law suits, environment and ecology, etc. etc.

The Hummer was on top of Maloney's black list. For Jesse, the GM monster was nothing less than a voracious fuel user, a polluter, a parking space glutton and a killer weapon (when colliding with other, smaller cars). He was even thinking of joining the *Hummer Haters* Internet site in which members gave their opinions about the militaristic vehicle. This web site was filled with scores of different pictures of people flipping the bird to the mammoth vehicles.

But, interestingly enough, during one such discussion, Newman also learned that the H2 represented a fantastic tax loophole. Apparently, because of an IRS miscalculation, business owners could deduct the entire cost of their $55,000 H2. For the highest tax brackets, the savings came close to $20,000! A rich entrepreneur could save more on his taxes by buying an H2 than purchasing an electric car. So much for the environment.

Was it possible that our successful cosmetic surgeon succumbed to the tax incentive in spite of his disgust for the vehicle? Philip knew Jesse too well to accept such a possibility. It was true that the man was sometimes pompous and sarcastic and -- more often than not -- a legend in his own mind. But he was a principled person. The Hummer was probably just a loaner from the dealership while Maloney's Cadillac was in the shop. This was a sneaky, but common, marketing system to make affluent customer drive their expensive cars and fall in love with them. But this did not mean that the person behind the H2 steering wheel this morning did not deserve a good teasing in the afternoon. Phil decided to serenade his friend at the end of the surgical schedule with a musical version of "If I had a Hummer...I would Hummer in the morning..."

After replacing the cap of the now full gas tank and putting his credit card back in his wallet, Newman peeked at his watch. There was still plenty of time left for both the post-op rounds and the pre-op patients visits.

He drove leisurely to the hospital. At such an early hour there was no point in hurrying. The physicians' car lot would not be crowded.

eighteen

The red Volkswagen swerved violently to avoid a collision, its driver clutching the wheel in a desperate attempt to avoid crashing into the massive oncoming vehicle, now rapidly advancing at an oblique angle. The maneuver only served to align the two perpendicularly as the Volkswagen's tires squealed, answered only by the increasing roar of a powerful engine.

The impact created an eardrum piercing violence of crushing metal and smashing glass, which drowned out the screaming hysteria of a female voice. The Volkswagen was hurled violently into a brick wall. The immense force had reduced the tiny vehicle to a twisted, unrecognizable simulation of a replica from an automobile junkyard compactor.

As the air cleared around the two vehicles, there was complete silence, as if no sound could penetrate the barrier of waves generated by that immense force. Suddenly, a low moan emanated from the crumpled vehicle followed by the frightened voices of bystanders. There weren't many voices. It was too early in the morning. But the deafening quietude did not last long. The dreadful accident took place outside the walls of the Soundedge Hospital. Within minutes, ambulance sirens filled the air.

nineteen

Phil was right. It was too early for the car lot to be crowded. But something unexpected was going on for sure. Instead of finding a vehicle parked in his usual spot by the door, he found Nora the admitting clerk standing there, gesticulating. She appeared nervous and panicky. Her hand movements signaled to the anesthesiologist to hurry up and come in quickly.

Philip parked the car next to the young woman and opened his driver side window. "What's going on, Nora?"

"Doctor Newman, the emergency room just called. They have a multiple *Code Blue*. There was a horrible two-car accident at the entrance of the nurses' parking lot a couple of minutes ago. It's total chaos! All I know, is that the victims are hospital employees. The ER needs help STAT!"

"OK, Nora. I'm going there right now. But if I'm not back on time to start the anesthesia, please let the OR supervisor know where I'm and why I'm there."

"I will, I will !"

Phil jumped out of his car and locked it by remote control. He sprinted as fast as he could, probably setting a new hospital speed record for the distance between the outpatient surgery entrance and the emergency room. Nora was right. In the ER, total pandemonium.. A woman and a man were being resuscitated on side by side ambulance stretchers, while another team was doing CPR on a second man, lying on a blanket on the floor. Blood everywhere.

The anesthesiologist decided to start by intubating the patient who appeared the most traumatized; the man on the ground. On his knees, Philip took over the *Ambu Bag* and continued the ventilation by mask, between the rhythmic closed chest massages provided by an EMT. When the laryngoscope and the endotracheal tubes arrived, Phil removed the mask, opened the mouth of the comatose accident victim and, after exposing the vocal cords, passed the tube without difficulty. To eliminate air leaks, the doctor quickly inflated the cuff inside the trachea and attached the open end of the tube to an automatic respirator. Now, with a stethoscope, he listened to the ventilated lungs. They were equally inflated.

Newman was now able to examine for the first time, the blood-smeared and no longer masked face of the comatose man.... my God! It was Bob Raye!

Despite all the efforts, the male nurse's pupils were dilated and his fingers blue. Intravenous lines were being started. A cardiologist was attaching EKG leads. Very little hope to bring him back, thought Philip. But no time for laments. Two more unconscious people were waiting.

Philip stood up and repeated the procedure on the woman. After the mask was off, the endotracheal tube in place and the automatic ventilation started, he recognized the features of her traumatized outline...it was Peg. Peggy Kane! And it was obvious that, between the squiggles caused by the closed chest massage, her EKG tracing was flat. The Soundedge operating room supervisor was dead.

The third accident victim did not need to be intubated for the moment. He was alive, moaning and fighting any attempt to put a mask on his face. It was Jesse. Jesse Maloney. His chest was moving unevenly. Probably a pneumothorax. He needed a chest x-ray and a chest tube. But Maloney's personal physician, who had just arrived, was taking over the decision making. Without wasting time, he decided on an immediate transfer by helicopter to the nearest open heart surgery center. The plastic surgeon appeared to have too much intra-thoracic trauma. Starting to x-ray him here before the move to a specialized hospital would be a dangerous waste of time.

So much for the "If I had a Hummer" serenade.

twenty

Philip was trying hard to remain a calm participant in the ER's inferno. It wasn't easy, even for an experienced physician. It's one thing not to be able to help dying strangers and another to lose, despite intensive efforts, people you know. Could he just go to the operating room now and continue his day in the gynecological room, like nothing has happened?

The emergency room secretary approached. "Dr Newman, could you talk on the telephone? Dr. Morris wants to know if you need help. He said that if you can't come to the phone, he will come here."

"I'll talk to him." The anesthesiologist walked to the desk and picked-up the receiver. "Good morning, boss. I suppose you know why I'm not in the operating room yet."

"Of course, Phil. Do you need help?"

"Send me God if you can. Only He could help. Our operating room supervisor and our male nurse are gone!"

"What exactly happened?"

"I have no idea, Ed. All I know is that I saw Maloney driving to the hospital in a Hummer this morning. From his extensive chest injuries, I deduce that he did not have his belts on. He presents typical signs of steering wheel trauma. Maybe he was busy talking on his cell phone. Maybe he was distracted. Apparently he plowed into Margaret's Volkswagen when she was making a left turn into the nurses' parking lot. Robert Raye was in Peggy's car. Do you happen to know what was he doing there?"

"Yes. Bob's car did not start yesterday evening and his mechanic could not come here until today. Margaret offered to give him a lift both ways. They live in the same neighborhood. Why was Jesse driving a Hummer?"

"I don't know. They are transferring him to the Saint Francis Hospital by helicopter. How many cases in Maloney's room today?" There was a short pause during which Philip heard the noise of shuffling paper.

"Four cases. Jay McMullen was supposed to give the anesthesia. I have no other cases for him for the moment but...wait...I think you had

71

enough for one day, Phil. Let me put Jay in your room and send you home. OK?"

"I would really appreciate it Ed. Thanks a million."

"Don't mention it. I hope the rest of your day improves. Enough is enough!"

Newman was more than happy to go home, but Ed Morris' hopes did not materialize. At 4:45 in the afternoon, Philip had a visitor.

twenty-one

Newman was about to get on the Internet when the front door bell rang. He hasn't checked his email in days. Leaving the computer on, Phil looked at his watch: 4:45 in the afternoon. Not only it was too early for Kyra to return from work, but, she always came in through the automatic garage door. If it couldn't be her, it must be somebody else. The mail already came. A neighbor? Fed Ex? UPS? DHL?

The man standing on the front step was well dressed and of a slight build. He had an attaché case in his left hand, legal-size envelope in his right and wore a dark suit with a dark tie. When the door opened, he immediately read the envelope's label in a loud voice, "Doctor Newman? Doctor Philip Newman?"

"Yes, I'm him. What can I do for you?"

Without saying another word, the man put the envelope in Phil's hands, turned around and left, walking toward his SUV parked in the driveway. The car had its engine running and its driver's side door was open. Despite his lack of previous experience, the anesthesiologist made a quick and correct diagnosis. But weren't subpoena servers supposed to say "you're being served," before leaving the premises?

After closing the front door, Philip opened the envelope, removed the inside papers and read the first page. He quickly realized what was going on. You have to be a masochist to be able to read word-by-word the many ways in which you're being described in a legal summons. They make a physician seem more like a murderer than a health care professional. The hospital where he practices? Not better than a slaughterhouse.

Newman smiled. A thought came to his mind. Did they ever dare serve Al Capone with those kind of papers? If the answer was *yes,* Capone's subpoena server probably came armed with a machine gun and surrounded by bodyguards, just to be safe.

It is rare for an anesthesiologist to be in a masochistic mood. Phil put the papers on his desk and sat down in front of the computer. He would read the accusations more completely, tomorrow. In any case, it was already too late now to inform his professional liability insurer *as soon as feasible* about the lawsuit, as stated in the insurance policy. And for sure nobody would be in the office at this time, ready to listen to his story, three minutes before closing. But the desire to tell somebody what had just happened, the need to share the bad news became more and more imperative. Where could he find instant professional reassurance? He decided to call Dr. Ross.

The phone rang once. "Arthur Ross speaking."

"Hi Art, Philip Newman calling."

"Good evening, Phil! What's cooking?"

"I'm being sued."

"I know the feeling Phil, but believe me, sooner or later it had to happen. Opening your door to your first subpoena server is exactly like doing your first parachute jump. Scary, very scary. But after the second time, the novelty wears off."

"Are you sure, Arthur?"

"Of course, my dear doctor. We live in a litigious society. Just try to accept it. You can cry and quit or you can smile and continue. In my time, I always chose to smile. As a matter of fact, during one of the multiple oil crises I sent an email to the White House on the subpoena serving subject. An energy saving proposal. Would you like to hear it?"

"Go ahead, Art."

"All I said was that, in our days, the American population seems divided into two major groups: One: the subpoena servers and two, the subpoena receivers. In major cities, subpoena serving is child's play. With dozens of subpoena receivers in each skyscraper, subpoena servers are able to do a day's work in minutes. But here, in suburbia, where the distance between subpoena receivers is measured in miles, subpoena serving is a gas-guzzling experience. Therefore, I proposed the installation of *Subpoena Centers* in shopping malls. Instead of driving like maniacs from door to door wasting gasoline, subpoena servers will now sit comfortably behind desks. By law, all citizens 18 or older will stop once a month during shopping and ask, 'Anything for me?'"

"And what did the White House had to say?"

"I'm still waiting for their answer. After all, it's been only eight years."

Philip giggled, loud enough to be heard. But he was in no laughing mood. He politely said good-bye to his ex-chief, wondering if Arthur Ross was suffering from an acute case of *humorrhagia*, or just a mild form of *Alzheimer's disease.*

What to do next? Who to speak to? After the restless Newman hung up the telephone receiver, he remembered that, when the doorbell rang, he was about to go on the Internet. By now, the computer had switched itself off. Phil quickly switched it back on and proceeded to check his Yahoo mail. The initial Mike Rooney message, the one mentioned by Doctor Morris, was still there, waiting to be read. Above it was a newer email from the same source. In it, the Los Angeles anesthesiologist was giving the first results of his *Tattoo removals under anesthesia, followed by complications or unexpected, unexplained operating room demise* survey.

So far there had been four cases reported, all in young people of both sexes. Three had fatal complications; the first in Durham, North Carolina, the second in Miami, Florida and the third in Seattle, Washington. The colors of the tattoo inks were not noted. No autopsies were performed and no explanations given as to why not. All three cases were followed by law-suits, all settled out-of-court. The fourth case in Austin, Texas, was a college swimmer returning tattooed from competition abroad. The prolonged paroxistic tachycardia, occurring soon after the injection of Lidocaine with 1/100000 epinephrine, forced the cancellation of the case. The patient recovered and, in the post-anesthesia care room, he acknowledged taking Ephedra to enhance athletic abilities. The young man returned Ephedra-free three weeks later, for an uneventful tattoo removal with skin graft.

There was also a fifth and very interesting letter, coming from an anesthesiologist in Detroit, Michigan. The good doctor was proposing widening the survey. He was still puzzled by an unexpected cardiac arrest in a young healthy woman, during cosmetic surgery on her nose, eighteen months ago. The autopsy refusal was followed by a lawsuit and a speedy out-of-court settlement. His question was: Why limit the discussion only to tattoo removals? He had created an *UNEXPECTED COMPLICATIONS AND/OR DEATH UNDER ANESTHESIA* web page. It was reserved to participating members and it could be entered by login and using a password. English speaking anesthesiologists from the entire world could use this forum to discuss and try to find explanations for all kind of mysterious operating room problems.

Philip decided to join right away, if not sooner. Never leave for tomorrow what you can do today. With what was going in his life at the moment, there was no guarantee that the next day he would remember to sign up. Was he over-reacting? Was every physician as obsessed and depressed as he was, after being sued? Maybe the new web page will give him the answer. He immediately sent an email address to the Detroit anesthesiologists with all his pertinent information.

During supper, Phil told Kyra the news. Being sued made him feel inferior, unworthy, discouraged, disheartened, ready to quit. She reassured him the best she could. In the United States today, if only the doctors who were never sued continued to practice medicine, there would be a handful of physicians and mile-long lines of patients outside their offices.

After dinner, Newman checked his email again. Detroit's answer was already there. The welcoming letter contained his login informations.

twenty-two

Until now, Kyra Newman thought she knew how to reassure her husband. In her demanding profession, the art of comforting was a must. Part of her pediatric nursing practice consisted of the daily dispensing of encouraging words, to worried parents. But today, she wished she could find a way to reassure herself. The spousal cheering up did not last. The man she was living with was just a shadow of the funny fellow she once knew. Doctor Philip Newman was no longer the person she married.

Phil was behaving like a robot. Withdrawn, dejected, quiet and obsessed. It all started the day after a stranger rang the bell and served him with process papers. A lawyer becomes acquainted with the medical profession the day he gets sick. A physician becomes acquainted with the judicial profession the day he gets sued. Both are depressing circumstances.

Her husband's daily grind hasn't changed. Early awakening, shower, shave, breakfast and the car trip to the hospital. No obvious changes. The legal doldrums appeared to have no influence on Phil's professional routines. The difference in her mate's behavior was apparent only after his working day in the operating room was over. Newman was spending an enormous amount of time in the hospital's library. He came home later and later and headed straight to his den to check the answering machine and his email. The bedroom was no longer the place for romance and love it once was. They no longer exchanged ideas and discussed plans for the future over relaxed meals in the dining room. Philip ate his meals faster and, when he wasn't eating or sleeping, he was either on the phone or on the Internet.

After the obligatory reporting of the lawsuit to his medical liability company, Phil was interviewed at length, by an insurance agent and by a defense lawyer. They came to his home on his evenings off. Kyra overheard most of the questions asked. It was clear that while a criminal is innocent until proved guilty, a doctor who loses a patient, is guilty until proven innocent. The written questionnaire left behind by the insurance people was enormous. It took Phil an entire weekend to complete it.

Kyra Newman was also faced with another problem. Before her marriage, she had promised Phil they would not have children. And she had kept her promise. Kyra took her birth control pills by the book, twenty one days a month. But she was starting to be concerned about being on the pill for so long. She knew all about the possible side effects; irregular menstrual bleeding, nauseas, headache, mood changes, weight gain and even a chance for dangerous blood clots. And these risks only increased as a woman aged. Why should a wife continue to take the pill when nothing was happening in the bedroom? Kyra needed to find a different contraceptive.

She decided to stop taking the birth control pills. No point on telling Phil right now. It would just stress him out some more. After all, Kyra Newman was scheduled to see her gynecologist for her annual checkup in a few days. What a better time to discuss contraceptive choices? In the meantime, the Internet seemed to be her husband's preferred form of birth control.

twenty-three

Philip Newman was quite aware that his moods and behavior had recently changed. Not for the better, for sure. Nevertheless, as is common in cases of acute depression, he was incapable of rational acceptance of reality. He reasoned defensively, "I still go to work every morning, just like before, and when I'm not on call, I still return home after work, just like before. Okay...so I spend more time on the Internet, less time at the dinner table, and no time at all on the tennis courts, but hey, this is no real cause for alarm...only a temporary schedule modification! Things will soon change!" He was convinced that slowly but surely, he would return to normalcy. "Starting today, I intend to stop by the tennis club during 'open-play' hours, as soon as I finish work, hit a few balls with the guys, and look for doubles partners."

His last afternoon case was a repeat TUR, a case for which he had been specifically requested. The trans-urethral resection of the prostate was to be performed on Scott Wilson, a 78-year-old very cooperative man, under spinal anesthesia. This patient preferred to remain awake again, during this, his third similar non-invasive procedure. For a person about to undergo surgery, Mr. Wilson was in a cheery mood. After all, his diagnosis was BPH -benign prostatic hypertrophy-rather than cancer. and, once again, he was able to reserve Dr. Newman for the anesthesia.

When Wilson spotted Phil entering the room he called out, "frequent flier Scott Wilson aboard and ready for takeoff!" He proved that he hadn't forgotten how his anesthesiologist liked to cheer him up, with his "welcome my Newman frequent flier" expression and with a touch of honest humor and a bright smile. The feeling was mutual.

"I should only be as sharp when I get to his age," Phil prayed silently. "This old guy knows all about the possible severe headache following the spinal, but he just shrugs it off. He accepts all the risks like one might, if one was playing poker. Follow the rules and you stack the odds in your favor." Wilson was convinced that with Newman present, the odds were already on his side. Hadn't the last two times been completely uneventful? Sitting up for the sterile injection, he had learned to bend his back forward as much as his 78-year-old dorsal stiffness allowed, so that the anesthesiologist could readily locate the best point of entrance - the space between the 3rd and the 4th lumbar vertebrae.

The sizes of medical needles are a total paradox. The smaller the number, the thicker the needle, the more painful the injection and, in the case of spinal taps, the greater the chance of a post-op spinal fluid leak. Such leaks, until they eventually stop, are very commonly followed by acute headaches. Therefore, a number 18 spinal needle represents a virtually guaranteed migraine-type throbbing. A number 20 needle still creates an enormous chance for a whopping postoperative headache. Thinner ones (from #22 up), are responsible for only a very slight possibility of a short-lasting, often painful experience.

Phil checked Scott Wilson's previous hospital charts. He had used a number 25 spinal needles each and every time. When you're able to use such a fine needle, there is no point in first numbing the skin with a subcutaneous anesthetic injection. This needle is shorter bu, of the same 25 caliber and, the burning sensation from the local anesthetic injection, is often more painful than the spinal tap itself.

Today, the anesthesia was uneventful again. With a good intravenous drip in place, the patient remained well hydrated, Phil sat him up, prepped the back with iodine and, after locating the 3d-4th lumbar intervertebral space through his sterile surgical gloves, he injected a hyperbaric mixture of 1% Pontocaine in 10% dextrose directly into the spinal canal. It was very important for the anesthetic mixture to always be heavier than the spinal fluid. Otherwise, the liquid could climb inside this spinal canal and, reaching the brain, paralyze the respiratory muscles. Once the medication was in, he laid the patient flat on his back followed by tilting of the OR table into a *Trendelenberg* (head down, legs up) position with his head comfortably elevated on one pillow. As soon as Mr. Wilson was no longer able to lift his legs, he was ready for surgery. Total analgesia from the waist down was now achieved.

Working rapidly, Phil brought the surgical table back to its horizontal position. After the circulating nurse raised the lower extremities up in stirrups, the urologist inserted his lubrified and sterilized cystoscope. The simple operation was now ready to be started. The surgical technique involved cutting away the invading parts of overgrown prostatic tissue with an electric knife, a *cautery*, in order to improve the urinary flow. All this was done directly under visual cystoscopic control. The procedure was performed via the urethral canal, with no need for a skin incision.

Scott Wilson was still feeling comfortable and pain-free upon his arrival at the post-anesthesia care unit. He knew that within a couple of hours he would be able to move his legs again, and the pain will start. But he was also aware that the longer he kept his head down on his pillow, the less chance he had of experiencing a spinal headache later-on. Aside from the possibility of that headache, the worst part of these surgical miseries was that nasty catheter sticking out of his penis. He had great sympathy for those mentally compromised patients, he encountered in hospital wards, who sometimes rip off their catheters. Ah! Today, he was resolved to bear the discomfort without asking the recovery room nurse for a pain killer. Those medications made him feel funny in his head. He also knew that the draining tube was destined to stay in place until all oozing of blood had ceased. Hopefully soon.

With no emergency cases added to his schedule, Phil was ready to leave. Today was the first day he had been able to prime himself for a return to the tennis court. For Phil, not feeling an urge to play tennis was almost as bad as not feeling like having sex, and let's face it, he hadn't much felt like satisfying either of the two obsessions lately. But, somehow, the desire for both was beginning to resurface. Only tennis was immediately available. His desire for tennis, was abetted by his obsessive behavior of keeping a spare tennis outfit in his hospital locker. Ten minutes after changing from his scrub suit to tennis attire, Dr. Newman's automobile was pulling into the Harbor Hills Golf and Tennis driveway.

"Doctor Newman! Just the man I was looking for..." the male voice came from behind his vehicle, the moment Phil started closing the car door. He recognized that this was the voice of Robert Barnes, life insurance agent and sometime tennis partner. He turned around to face the caller.

"Mr. Barnes, I presume. Looking for a good tennis player to hit a few balls?"

"Yeah, but I'll play with you anyway, Phil," Barnes quipped. "I gather you're available. Wanna play a couple of sets? I'd like to have a little talk with you when we're done. Got some questions to ask. Treat you to a beer. Okay?"

They played a shorter match than planned. Tennis is less fun when the mind of one of the players is not on the game. Towels in hand, they approached the bar. "Heineken, Phil?"

"Heineken will be great, Bob. What's the subject of our conversation?"

"Questions about one of your ex-patients, James Walker. He died under anesthesia."

"What,? The whole world knows about my cardiac arrest case?"

Robert Barnes waited quietly for the beer to be served and for the waitress to leave the table. "Not the entire world knows the story, Phil, but I do. I was his life insurance agent."

"A nineteen year old kid carried life insurance?"

"It does happen now and then. Usually it's given as a gift from somebody in the family. Most often, it's a present from the parents and occasionally, an endowment from the grandparents. It's a thoughtful offering, especially when the young person has a significant other in his or her life, or is engaged to be married. Anyway, why not? After all, the younger the insured, the cheaper the cost."

"What kind of insurance did he carry and for how much?"

"I really don't have the right to disclose that information Phil, unless you promise me that everything we discuss here will remain just between us...completely confidential, and if you don't mind, I'd like to make it a mutual exchange because my insurance company is interested in asking you a few probably restricted questions. Okay?"

"Okay, I promise, Bob." Phil replied playfully placing his right hand over his left chest.

"Well," Barnes offered, "the policy purchased in James Walker's name was term insurance, in the amount of $200,000. It was bought three months before his death. The life insurance company is puzzled because, statistically speaking, young people die mainly in car and sport accidents or when they commit suicide. Not on operating room tables. Why did he die, Phil?"

"I wish I knew, Bob. We have a few theories but nothing is sure yet. There was no post-mortem. His father refused the autopsy for religious reasons, but his religion doesn't stop him from suing us for medical malpractice. Moreover, when it comes to statistics, don't believe a word. They can be interpreted in all sorts of ways."

"What do you mean by that?"

"Statistically speaking, if I get sick, and I want to be safe, I should stay home in my own bed. I bought my bed a dozen years ago and, so far, nobody died in it. More Americans die in a hospital bed than in virtually any other location. Of course, even more people die in intensive care and coronary care units than in regular hospital wards."

"I know you're joking, Phil, but at least, I do understand now what you mean by statistical interpretations."

"Tell me, will the family of the deceased collect the insurance money if the insured commits suicide?"

"It all depends on the policy. Some companies simply exclude suicide completely, some have two year exclusions during which they can investigate the legitimacy of the action, some won't pay unless six or eight months have passed since the policy was written, and some allow for certain exceptions wherein it's obvious that the policy wasn't taken out for that purpose. Our company uses the two-year delay clause so they can make sure that no hanky-panky took place. In this case, there seems to be little suspicion of anything like that, especially since the policy amount was only $200,000 and death occurred during surgery. Still, if we can save two hundred grand, why not? Anyway, how come you're asking about suicide? You think there's more to this than meets the eye, or are you just searching for ways to cover your ass? How much are you getting stiffed for?"

"Two million dollars. I'd rather not settle, but I'm being squeezed. They just want to get out with the least damage, both financially and public image. You're in the insurance business Bob. Any idea what kind of settlement they can manage? Ah, the hell with it, who cares? Now it's all in the hands of my medical liability insurance company's lawyers and their lawyers."

Phil decided not to disclose the testicular carcinoma diagnosis. Even in confidential situations, there must be some medical ethical limits. Nevertheless, what he learned from Robert Barnes today was very interesting. He couldn't wait to pass along the information to Mike

Rooney and the other members of the *Anesthesiology Web Page*, of course, without disclosing its source. Newman decided to take advantage of the presence of his insurance agent and of this rare moment of confidentiality: "May I ask you an Insurance question, Bob?"

"Shoot! What's on your mind?

"Is there a way to find out if somebody carries life insurance?"

"Life insurance? Listen Phil, these days you can find out just about anything you want to know, about anybody you want but, you've got to be willing to perform some legal maneuvers. If the insured is still alive, and if you're in possession of some of his particulars, it's fairly easy. It just takes a bit of savvy and acting ability. The keys are the Social Security Number, along with the exact name, address, and birth date. You can get such info from a person's medical records. Then all you have to do is call the major insurance companies in your area and make believe you're him. Pretend you lost your insurance policies. They'll take it from there and you've got it made."

"Wow! As easy as that? And if the person is dead?"

"Even easier then. All you have to know in that case, are the social security number of the deceased and the telephone number of your State Tax Bureau."

"Life insurance benefits are taxable?"

"Of course not but, when a person dies, the State is always the first to know if this person had life insurance. The State has *first refusal rights*. If the deceased owes tax money, the State is the first to collect. That's why anybody can call them, give the social security number of the deceased, represent themselves as kin to the deceased and inquire if the defunct owed tax money. The State will willingly give them all the necessary information."

"That's totally incredible, Bob. I never dreamed it could be that easy. I just wonder if I'd have the guts to pull off something like that."

"If you can't bring yourself to fake it, there is another method. It costs a little money, but you only have to do one thing, get that social security number from the chart."

"You mean, use a private eye?"

"You guess it! Just hire one of those private investigation companies. Give them the Social Security Number, and they'll find you anything you want...even unlisted phone numbers, if you so desire. And believe me, Phil; it's much easier to get life insurance informations, than unlisted phone numbers."

"How do you go about finding a private eye?"

"Where else? They're all over the Internet. Just type 'private investigator' on Google or any other search engine. You'll see. They're a dime a dozen."

"Yeah! I might have known."

"Listen Phil, what's with all this sudden interest in getting personal info about people? You mind filling me in?"

"Sure Bob. Nothing more than a suspicion that something strange is going on. A few of us got curious about the similarities we noticed between the Walker case and several others in various parts of the country. We've formed a group of concerned anesthesiologists trying to understand exactly what's happening. We're attempting to solve, if possible, the mystery of unexpected, unexplained operating room fatalities. We have a forum on the Internet. As soon as I get home tonight, I'll put all the information I received from you today on our web page, without disclosing the source, of course. Okay with you, Bob?"

"Phil, do anything you want. Just keep me out of it!"

"Thank you, Bob! I'm much obliged. I'm going to take off now. Please give my regards to your wife."

"You too, Phil."

Without being able to understand exactly why, Phil went home in a better mood. He had a strong feeling that this life insurance information would help unravel this all consuming mystery.

Kyra immediately saw the difference in her husband. He was chatty on arrival, talkative during supper and, for a change, took his time eating. He even waited for her to finish her coffee, before he left the table to go on the Internet.

Upon arrival at the operating room the next morning, Phil was informed that his first case had been delegated to another anesthesiologist. "You're wanted at the hospital administrator's office, Phil."

"As if I don't have enough problems," he murmured to himself, and then headed for the elevator. His lightened mood of the previous evening was gone in an instant. When entering the administrative suite., he felt sweaty. He grabbed a couple of tissues from a Kleenex box on the side table and wiped his forehead and scalp.

"Have a seat Dr. Newman. Mr. Halliday will see you in a few minutes."

If he was looking for reassurance, the waiting was no help. The moisture on his forehead continued to plague him to the point that he was forced to use his cotton handkerchief. The *few minutes* seemed like angst ridden hours. He looked at his watch frequently. The agonizing twenty-two minute wait had transformed his confidence from that of a seasoned professional to a neophyte about to embark on a new venture into an alien world.

"Step right in, doctor," Halliday's secretary announced, pointing unnecessarily to the administrator's door. Lord knows, I've been here before, he thought.

"Hi, Phil!" The upbeat welcoming tone of Halliday's voice immediately reversed the stifling atmosphere of the moment before.

"Hi, Jack! What's up?" Phil seemed completely recovered. It's amazing what a pleasant greeting can do, to alter a mood.

"I'm sure you must have guessed by now. They're suing us for 100 millions but they are ready to settle out-of-court, for much less. If we go to trial, some do-gooder jury will probably cream us. The insurance company is insisting that we settle, and they want everyone else involved to do the same. We're going along with it, to avoid a reputation-ruining trial in the media. We're asking everyone involved to go along with us. Okay?"

"Jack, I appreciate your point of view, but I've been mulling this in my mind, trying to figure out why I can't seem to get over the idea that there's more to this case than meets the eye. Until I'll be able to get my thoughts sorted out, I can't accept the idea of merely walking away from what happened. Something fishy is going on. I want to know what it is."

"Phil, I talked to Margaret Kane and Bob Raye before they died. The suing SOBs are going after everyone and everything in sight. Peg and Bob were both cited for negligence. Obviously it's not true, but they knew damn well that the insurance companies would want to settle and get out of this, as fast as possible, for as little as possible. Margaret didn't mince her words. She said she didn't do anything wrong and was not about to let those bastards say that she did. Now I have to convince her estate administrator to agree to settle. I'm sure her insurance company is also going to apply plenty of pressure. I'm not worried about Bob's estate. He was more agreeable, and I don't think his insurance company will have any trouble getting their way. Phil, you are aware I hope, that your medical liability insurance company is going to push you against the wall, trying to convince you to settle. You'll simplify your life by trying to forget about those suspicions, and go along with us."

"Jack, I need some time to think things over. The idea of settling goes against my grain. Furthermore, I really feel as if something else, something much more serious is going on. I just can't quite put my finger on it yet."

"Okay, Phil! But please don't push things too far. The hospital can't afford to have the sharks get their teeth into this thing. You're well aware that we're in severe financial straits. Something like this could shove us off the edge."

"I'll keep that in mind. I just need the time to sort things out. I'll keep you posted, okay?"

"Okay. See you at Margaret's funeral. You know that Bob's being buried in his hometown?"

"Yeah, I know. Did you go to the wake?"

"No. I was not able to."

"Me neither, but I'm going tomorrow morning to the funeral. Are you coming too?"

"Of course, Phil. See you at the funeral."

twenty-four

It was not a problem for Philip to take the day off the morning of the funeral. None of the anesthesiologists in the group were away at the moment. The obsequies were scheduled for 10:00 AM. The ride to the Calvary Cemetery should not take longer than 45 minutes. He decided to leave the house around nine, in order to allow some extra time for the always unpredictable Long Island traffic.

Newman was not looking forward to the funeral, but he was aware that his presence there was not optional. Before she left for work, Kyra left his black suit, a white shirt and a black tie ready on a bedroom chair. She knew that, left on his own, the man who spends half of his life wearing scrub suits, would have a problem putting together an appropriate outfit to wear to such a sad occasion.

Phil was examining the knot of his tie in the bathroom mirror, when the phone rang.. He immediately recognized the voice of Ed Morris. "Good morning, chief. What's up?"

"I need you as soon as possible, Phil. Room three. A bleeding gunshot wound. All other operating rooms are busy with long cases. You're my only solution. If there is such a thing as an afterlife, our poor deceased OR supervisor would understand your absence at her burial. I'm really sorry!

"No problem, Ed. I'm on my way."

Philip removed the now useless tie, placed it back on the bedroom chair and, grabbing his jacket, decided to drive to the hospital dressed in his black suit. With the white shirt comfortably open, he jumped in his car. The street was temporarily blocked by the private sanitation truck, driving in the middle of the road, collecting refuse from both sides. No point to beep the horn. One more minute will not change the world. Anesthesiologists are used to hurry up and wait.

Not being able to go to an important appointment was just one of the drawbacks of the *gaspassers* profession. For him, today, it was a funeral. Some of his younger colleagues missed the delivery of their own babies. The young Jay McMullen took one week off during his pregnant wife *due date,* only to become involved in the vaginal delivery of a lady who decided to have a baby at exactly the same time Mrs. McMullen did.

As a rule, ambulances always call the hospitals ahead to inquire things like: "Is there a neurosurgeon available? Do you have a vascular surgeon in the house?" If the reply is negative, they take their wounded to another institution. But they never call and ask if an anesthesiologist is free to take over the case. This isn't their problem. The anesthesia department will have to manage.

By the time Newman changed to surgical attire, a voice on the intercom announced that the case was ready to start.

The badly wounded patient was already on the OR table in room three. No time for pre-op evaluation. No time to meet the next-of-kin. Phil ran to his designated surgical suite where he found his young male patient screaming. The bandages on his injured left thigh were soaked in blood. The blood was lost before his local circulation was stopped by a well applied tourniquet. But a limb cannot remain without its blood supply forever. His femoral artery had to be quickly repaired to allow the removal of the tourniquet and the repair of the painful open fracture of the femur.

The patient's chart waiting on the anesthesia machine. According to it, the name of this eighteen year old suffering patient was Carlos Gonzales. The injured teenager was in too much pain to answer questions. It took Newman less than a minute to ascertain that all the instruments, the tubes and drugs he needed were available. He proceeded with a rapid induction of anesthesia through the already existing intravenous line, followed by a *crash intubation.* Such a super-fast introduction of the endotracheal tube in the windpipe is necessary when the emptiness of the stomach cannot be assessed. It is better to take a chance of traumatizing the larynx or breaking a tooth rather than letting the patient drown in his own vomit.

With the shooting victim now asleep and his airway secured, the anesthesiologist finally could acquaint himself with the case. Carlos Gonzales had been crossed-matched in the emergency room for four units of blood which would soon be available. He was shot in the parking lot of a twenty-four hour pharmacy and, despite the intense hemorrhage occurring before the application of the tourniquet, his vital signs remained stable, throughout the ambulance ride and in the ER. The EMTs did a fantastic job.

Drs. Joseph Rosenberg and Norman Kramer appeared. They were scrubbed, arms elevated and dripping, ready to be toweled, gowned and start the case. First, Rosenberg will repair the artery and, later on, Kramer will take care of the bone.

At the start of the case, the orthopedic surgeon was in a chatty mood. After all, during the arterial repair, he was just a retractor holding surgical assistant free to talk. He knew exactly what had happened in the parking lot. The police officer handling the case was an old ER acquaintance. The young patient was shot by a crippled Vietnam veteran over a handicapped parking space dispute.

Apparently the young Gonzales, alone in his disabled grandfather's car, got to the handicapped space in front of the pharmacy entrance before the amputee Veteran. The Vietnam vet stopped his car just behind and shouted at the teenager to move. Without saying a word, Carlos Gonzales attached his grandfather's *Handicapped* placard to the rear-view mirror and went inside the pharmacy. On his return, the ex-marine was waiting, driver-side window open, gun in hand. After the shooting, the Veteran awaited quietly the arrival of the police officers. Surrendering his weapon, the vet told the cops in a calm voice: "I hate liars! From now on, this kid will be able to use the *Handicapped Parking* without having to lie..."

The left femoral artery repair and the open reduction with insertion of a metallic plate in the left femur took five hours. Plenty of time for Philip Newman to ruminate.

Phil knew the angry feeling one gets when one sees a young healthy person park in a handicapped space, while honest people are forced to look for far away available spaces. Where is the police enforcement? Why isn't there a picture of the disabled permit holder, on the handicapped placard? Getting angry is probably normal. But shooting somebody? Maiming a person for a lousy handicapped parking spot? Is *Parking Rage* a chapter of *Road Rage* or a book on its own?

The case went smoothly. The anesthesia was lightened during the application of the long-leg cast. The vital signs remained stable during the entire procedure. No blood transfusions needed. After extubation,

Newman inspected the teeth of the still asleep patient only to observe a tiny chip in the left upper incisor. He made a note on the anesthesia record. Philip Newman MD refused to solve such problems with a nail file like some of his colleagues did..

Phil brought the now awakening teenager to the post-anesthesia care unit and wrote "STAT hemoglobin" on the physician's orders sheet. He would call later for the results and decide if the patient needed blood.

Newman left the recovery room still annoyed with himself. That chipped tooth would spoil the rest of his day. He hated to feel imperfect.

But the self-maintained annoyance did not have a chance to linger. Ed Morris caught up with him in the corridor. "Sorry, Phil. I need you again."

The urgent case was an 81 year old moribund man brought over to the emergency room, by ambulance, from a local nursing home. On the cover of his hospital chart was clearly marked DNR. Philip was aware that the right to elect not to be revived when the heart stops, being present on the *Do Not Resuscitate* list, did not imply the right to an assisted suicide.

The sick man's face appeared jaundiced and, despite the presence of a decompressing *Levine tube* in his nose , his abdomen was still obviously distended. Extruding from his right nostril, the transparent naso-gastric tube was secured to the bluish tinged nose by strands of pink adhesive tape. One end was obviously in the stomach, the other attached to the plastic hose of an already half-full suction bottle. By his non-stop moaning it was clear that the man was in acute distress. To relieve the very painful intestinal obstruction, an emergency colostomy had to be performed as soon as possible.

His medical diagnosis was hopeless: *terminal metastatic rectal cancer,* but very few surgeons and anesthesiologists accept taking care of people in painful agony, while their names are present on the DNR list. The *Do Not Resuscitate* order has to be rescinded before a patient's arrival in the operating room. Newman was one of them. He could not imagine losing a human being on the OR table and standing-by, doing nothing. Keeping a hands-off policy, allowing an individual to die without trying to help during surgery, was neither taught in medical schools, nor during the Anesthesiology residency years. And in top of it, like most American physicians, Phil was also aware of the legal implications of such negative OR outcome. The definition of *Do Not Resuscitate* is a specific order not to revive patients artificially, if they succumb to their terminal illnesses. But, inside a surgical suite, "Crossing the Bar," like Tennyson liked to define death, could always be considered a case of surgical or anesthesia malpractice.

Was it possible that way before the advent of legal contingency fees, the English poet with his "Crossing the Bar" literary definition, already knew how hungry some of the members of the American Bar Association are going to be?

There was no point in explaining the need to temporarily revoke the DNR order, to the agonizing patient. He obviously lacked decision making capacity. But the next of kin, his wife, a tall, very elegant white-haired lady, seemed very understanding. After receiving all the necessary explanations and, after being reassured that immediately after surgery the DNR. order will be reinstated, she joined Philip in signing the necessary papers, without protesting.

The operation was fast and simple. Following a careful irrigation of the naso-gastric tube, a mild intravenous sedation was started, 100% oxygen administered by mask and a local anesthetic injected. Less than half an hour later, the moribund was in his post-anesthesia care bed, with a colostomy bag attached by a belt to his abdomen. The DNR order was immediately reinstated and signed by his wife and by Dr. Newman.

Leaving the recovery room, Phil couldn't stop thinking about the James Walker case again: here we have an old hopeless moribund alive while a previously healthy young man is as dead as a doornail.

Life is not fair!

twenty-five

Newman made the decision to not discuss his day-to-day professional problems, with other anonymous Internet correspondents. After all, this anesthesia website was created only in the hope of solving the mystery of unexpected and unexplained operating room deaths. The physicians visiting here were surely not interested in reading individual paranoid complaints.

As soon as the web page opened up, Philip clicked on the link marked *NEW REPORTED CASES.* There were two new reports, on a couple of not so new occurrences. Both cardiac arrests took place just over a year ago in Nebraska. One in Omaha, the other one in Lincoln. The Nebraskan anesthesiology groups found out only recently about the investigation. They were not able to furnish too many details. Both fatalities were young. One male, one female. Both surgical operations for removal of unwanted tattoos. The colors of the tattoo inks were not marked on the hospital charts and, therefore not available. Neither were the dollar amounts of the out-of-court settlements. Both autopsy requests were refused for religious reasons.

As soon as he finished reading, Phil started to type his latest information and suspicions. He explained why it could be very interesting and important to find out how many of the families of those young deceased collected life insurance, in addition to the medical malpractice settlements. After describing how life insurance informations could be obtained, Newman concluded that the simplest way was to copy the Social Security Numbers from the hospital charts and pass them along to hired private detectives. It was not too expensive, he added.

Without disclosing names, Phil explained how he accidentally discovered in his patient's case there was an undisclosed history of cancer. The family of the deceased was now trying to collect double insurance: term life and medical liability. Was this true in other cases?

"Of course," Newman continued to type, *"I'm aware that it is impossible to find out after the fact, if any others of the defunct young patients also suffered from incurable diseases. But it is important to remember that, until now, the possible common links in all our cases*

were either drug interaction or poisonous tattoo inks. The recent disclosures of non-lethal Ephedra complications during anesthesia and of fatal operating room outcomes in cases not related to tattoo removals, are somehow changing the outlook. The refusal of autopsy seems to be, for the time being, the only perfect connection. Could the avoidance of a possible discovery of pre-existing malignancies be the best explanation for such generalized denials of postmortem examinations?"

"My latest hypothesis is the possibility of quiet suicide help either from the Hemlock Society or from some other similar groups." He advised all the anesthesiologists to read the *Final Exit* book as a reference. In its time, it was a *Hemlock Society* bestseller. Written by their founder Derek Humphry, the book explains all *"the practicalities of self-deliverance and assisted suicide for the dying."*

"Jack Kevorkian put 'doctor assisted suicide' under the microscope," opined Phil. *"So why not replace it with some secret and safer advice, on how to kill yourself under anesthesia? Maybe young cancer patients who don't have pre-existing surgical problems (to justify the necessity of anesthesia), are advised to have their arms tattooed and, later on, to take advantage of the surgical removal and do themselves in.".*

"It is horrible to die young, of course, but if your disease forces you to decide ending your life, why end it for nothing? Perhaps some of the insurance money quietly benefited the Hemlock Society. Who knows?"

On finishing his account, Newman remarked that, as far as he knew, there were no reported cases of unexpected, unexplained death under anesthesia, in the state of Oregon. Maybe something to do with the fact that the *Hemlock Society* headquarters are located in Eugene? Were they playing it safe?

As soon as the web page was closed, Phil checked his email. Spam, spam and more spam. Penile enlargement devices and get rich quick schemes with the occasional *Hi* as a subject line, from an unknown sender. After erasing all the bulk mail, Phil clicked on *compose mail*. He decided to write a short note advising Mike Rooney to read the latest news on the *Anesthesiology Web Page*.

But, after switching his computer off, Philip decided to call Rooney on his mobile phone, After all, Phil had absolutely no idea how often Mike checked his email. Nobody picked-up. Dr. Rooney's voice mail came on and, Newman left a verbal message reiterating what he had just wrote to him by email.

twenty-six

Is NO NEWS always GOOD NEWS? Since the posting of his last Internet entry, Philip Newman had checked his answering machine, his email and the *Anesthesiology Web Page* as often as he was able to. Nothing. No news the day before, nothing yesterday and, so far, no news today.

Deep down he knew that things seldom happened as fast as he would like them to happen. But such knowledge did not stop him from compulsively checking and rechecking. He was even checking his answering machine from the operating room now. Only during easy cases, of course. All he had to do was press 9 on the OR telephone to obtain an outside *local calls only* line. Other anesthesiologists spoke daily, during surgical cases, with their stockbrokers on toll-free numbers. Not Newman. He never did such things before the events. His patients deserved total attention.

Today, he was in charge of the anesthesia for light orthopedic cases. Two arthroscopies-arthroplasties of the knees under general, followed by two carpal tunnel releases, under regional. The hand operations consisted of the simple decompression of the median nerve pinched by an inflamed transverse carpal ligament. Such *tenosynovitis* occurs mainly in younger people, more often woman than men, who repeat the same movements perpetually.

In these type of cases, *intravenous regional anesthesia* was the preferred method. Philip did not learn the technique during his years in a teaching hospital. He mastered the intravascular approach while already in private practice.

The technique was simple: the good arm was used for the intravenous infusion and for the blood pressure monitoring machine.

The side about to be operated on, received an intravenous cannula (attached to a syringe extension) and a deflated tourniquet. After most of the venous blood was ejected by the rolling of a tight elastic bandage, on the vertically elevated arm, from fingertips down, the tourniquet was inflated and the bandage removed. The veins of the now pale and anemic looking arm were ready to be filled with a diluted local anesthetic solution.

Unlike some delicate and often difficult to obtain nerve blocks, this system worked each and every time. There was only one important requirement; the surgical release of the carpal tunnel had to be performed in no longer than an hour. A tourniquet cannot be left inflated in place longer than 60 minutes, without the risk of gangrene. This was probably the reason why the method was seldom taught in teaching hospitals. Surgical residents in training, took longer to do the procedure. Much longer.

During the first of the two hand operations, Phil called his home phone twice. Both times he hung up after the third ring. More than one ring meant *"no new messages."* At the end of the case and after the orthopedic surgeon finished applying the sterile dressings, it was time to slowly and intermittently deflate the tourniquet. A fast release of pressure allows some of the non absorbed local anesthetic to enter the blood stream *en-masse*, causing a fainting feeling when reaching the brain. Newman learned that the hard way. During the first few intravenous regional anesthetics he administered, he found out that what he thought at the time to be a *slow release* was not slow enough. Practice makes perfect.

Phil called home again during the second carpal tunnel release. This time, he heard Kyra's cheerful message immediately after the first ring. *"You have reached the Newman residence. Please leave a message after the beep!"* Somebody had called.

Philip pressed star-7 and, after the robotic *YOU HAVE ONE MESSAGE,* he pressed star-1 as required. Right away, he recognized the voice of the Los Angeles anesthesiologist: "Hi Phil, this is Mike. Mike Rooney. As per your advice I hired a private investigator. Not only did the detective quickly discover that our cardiac arrest patient carried term life insurance just like yours, but he was also able to find, and put me in contact with, his out-of-town family physician. This allowed me to check on possible pre-existing conditions. There were none. The kid was healthy, had regular check-ups, received all his vaccinations and apparently traveled a lot. One interesting point: before his last trip, the trip from which he returned tattooed, he asked to be vaccinated for

Hepatitis A and B, Typhoid, Encephalitis and he also requested a polio booster. What do you think? Please give me a call when you have a chance."

Phil was rattled. Polio-boosters he understood. But Hepatitis? Encephalitis? Typhoid? Those facts were surely important. He would have to review some of the long forgotten *Medical Epidemiology* manuals.

It was the end of his last case. Mrs. Rodriguez, his last patient, complained of *slight unpleasant dizziness* following the tourniquet deflation, but it did not prevent her from smiling, relieved that it was over. After all, the Doctor had made her aware of the possibility of that side-effect during his pre-op visit. Such cooperative surgical patients who knew exactly what to expect, always reminded him of the late Peggy Kane and her classic phrase used during OR Personnel training: *"And don't forget! An informed healthcare consumer is our best customer."*

During the transfer on the mobile stretcher from the OR to the recovery room, Newman left the post-op patient flat on her back, head elevated on one pillow, bandaged arm elevated on two. On arrival, he instructed the recovery room nurse to lift her to a sitting position only when the dizziness had stopped. Then he turned back toward Mrs. Rodriguez. "Is your husband in the waiting room? I would like to tell him what a super trooper you are!"

"Don't bother, doctor! I sent him to work. They will call him when it's time to pick me up. He's only half an hour away."

"You're the boss, Mrs. Rodriguez. I ordered pain medications as needed. Thank you for flying with us!"

This made her smile.

"Dr. Newman, we need you!" The alarmed voice came from the other end of the post anesthesia care unit. Phil walked as fast as he could. With the exception of a *Code Blue,* it was not recommended that recovering surgical patients observe their physicians running.

He found an unconscious obese male on a hospital trolley, vomiting. Probably PONV, the dreaded *Post Operative Nausea and Vomiting.* The curtains were pulled closed to prevent other patients from seeing what was going on. One nurse was holding his head turned to the side, while a second nurse was attempting to suction his mouth and throat. Coming from his left nostril, a bile-filled naso-gastric tube was attached to a half filled suction bottle. His lips were blue.

Dr. Newman spoke fast. "This patient is in laryngospasm. It's possible that he aspirated. I have to intubate him STAT. I need a laryngoscope, a 9 millimeter, cuffed endotracheal tube and an Ambu bag with oxygen attached. Does he have any capped teeth or dentures?"

"I don't know. Should I check his chart?" The resuscitation tray was ready.

"No time for that!" The anesthesiologist straightened the patient's head and removed the pillow. Extending the head makes the oro-tracheal intubation easier. But in obese people with thick, short necks, such a maneuver is difficult, if not impossible, no matter what. It was going to be a tough intubation!

Philip opened the gurgling foaming mouth and quickly suctioned inside as deeply as possible. He then inserted the lighted laryngoscope and continued to suction under direct vision. No vocal cords, no trachea in sight! The tip of the larynx became visible only after he asked a nurse to push down on the Adam's Apple.

"I need a smaller tube. A cuffed 8 millimeters with a flexible stylet inside. Lots of lubrication please!" Newman was finally able to intubate the patient. He quickly inflated the cuff to eliminate leaks, suctioned through the tube and, after attaching it to the Ambu bag, he began to ventilate the patient.

As soon as the bluish lips pinked up, Philip exchanged the Ambu for an automatic ventilator. After that he listened to both patient's lungs, just to make sure that the tube was in the correct, above the carina, position. The carina is the bifurcation point where one trachea becomes two bronchi. Assured that both lungs were equally ventilated, the anesthesiologist asked for a bite-block to prevent the unconscious patient from chewing on his lifesaving endotracheal tube.

Opening the mouth with the help of a tongue blade, Phil observed a dental gap. Part of the upper left incisor was missing. The patient was now pink, his EKG was showing regular tachycardia but the fast heart rate was nicely slowing down. His blood pressure was almost back to normal. Time to check the chart.

Name: Martin Kennedy. Age 60. Operation: *cholecystectomy, operative cholangiogram and common duct exploration.* A laparoscopy was first attempted but, as is sometimes necessary in very obese patients, a transverse abdominal incision became necessary to allow the removal of the gall bladder and of any existing stones in the bile duct.

The anesthesiologist on the case was Jay McMullen. Newman checked the pre-anesthetic notes: *"capped upper left incisor."* There were no post-operative notes yet. Phil read the operative schedule on the bulletin board. This was Jay's last case. The next operation was cancelled. The young anesthesiologist had probably gone home. But who broke the capped tooth, McMullen or Newman? Philip called both Jay's numbers, cell phone and home, to no avail. He left similar messages on both. After writing the complete description of the PONV management on patient's chart, Phil went to the waiting room to inform Kennedy's next of kin about the events. On the way, he waved to Mrs. Rodriguez, who was now sitting up, smiling, ready to go home.

On listening to the news, the waiting wife, the son and the daughter in law were in shock. "But less than an hour ago Dr. McMullen told us that everything was fine! Now, instead of telling us that Martin went back to his bed upstairs, you come here to tell us that he is on a ventilator and one of his teeth is missing? Who the hell are you? What did you do to him? You're going to hear from us, Doctor!"

Newman remained speechless. He could not find words to reply to such an unexpected verbal attack. He understood now better why Dr. Ross, his ex-chief, relied on his CYA practice of defensive medicine before retirement age.

Philip turned around and left without saying another word. Should he preventively call his medical liability insurer? He only just spoke to them about the Walker case, a short time ago. Was he becoming a bad insurable risk? How high was his insurance rate going to go?

He went to bed ruminating.

The phone rang just before midnight.

twenty-seven

The following day, his first case was now an added semi-emergency. A young person whose motorcycle helmet protected his skull, but not the rest of his head, from the consequences of a bad accident. A very lucky young man. If you drive fast on a two-wheeler and collide with a four-wheeler, you count your blessings when only your jaw is broken. After speaking to Edward Morris, Sanford Jacobson, the oral surgeon, received permission to *squeeze* the case in, ahead of the schedule. He was the one calling Newman at night, from the emergency room.

"Good evening, Phil. Sorry to call you so late! Jacobson here."

"I recognize your voice anywhere Sandy! What's cooking?"

"I'm in the ER with a fracture-dislocation of a jaw. A Harley-Davidson injury, on a full stomach. Not enough of an emergency to operate now, but we also can't wait too long. I have to wire him in the next eight hours. I already spoke to your chief. He put me in your room, first thing in the morning. The surgeon who will now follow me, was happy to start later. Could we begin at 7 o'clock instead of 7:30?"

"Did he get neuro clearance?"

"Yes, the neurologists saw him. No fractured skull. His brains are fine."

"In that case, seven it is! Make sure that the emergency room nurse phones the anesthesiologist on call, to come and see the patient and leave some pre-op orders."

"Ed Morris promised to take care of that."

"Great! How old is your accident victim?"

"Early twenties and otherwise healthy."

"OK, Sandy. I'll see you at seven."

"I will need a nasal intubation."

"Why? Are you going to wire both the maxilla and the mandible?"

"Yes."

"Do you think he will be able to swallow some Sudafed in the morning?"

"I don't think so."

"No problem. In this case, could you please order a nasal vaso-constrictor? Have them spray both nostrils with a decongestant an hour before surgery."

"Afrin?"

"Afrin will be great. See you at 7:00. Please don't be late."

"Me, late?" Jacobson laughed on the phone. "I'm never late! You forgot who you are talking to."

"Of course, Sir! I know exactly who I'm talking to. I never forget such things. This is probably why I'm asking you not to be late! See you tomorrow, Sandy." Phil was still grinning as he hung up the phone.

The next morning, Newman arrived at the hospital forty minutes earlier than usual. He wanted to check on Martin Kennedy, his PONV patient from yesterday, before starting his cases. Phil checked the hospital computer at the front desk. Good news. Kennedy had no need for the intensive care unit. He had been moved from the post-anesthesia care unit, directly to the fourth floor, a regular surgical unit.

The PONV notation always made Philip smile. This funny abbreviation had been invented over a dozen years ago by the drug industry and it stuck. They were offering more and more injectable products to protect against *Post Operative Nausea and Vomiting* and God only knew how effective they really were. Newman didn't. People still get sick in the recovery room, especially after intra-abdominal surgery. Are they vomiting less with PONV medications than without them? It was impossible to know. In the era of *"Ask Your Doctor"* TV commercials, as soon as a drug is approved by the Federal Drugs Administration and recommended by the pharmaceutical industry, few physicians have the guts not to offer it to their patients.

Philip Newman was still looking at the computer screen when he felt a tap on his shoulder. He turned around. It was Jay McMullen.

"Thank you for yesterday, Phil!"

"Don't mention it, Jay. I was just going up to see your patient now. I see he's on a regular floor. Thank God! How is he doing?"

"He's doing great. I spent most of the night with him. After receiving your message, I came back immediately. Sorry I didn't return your call, but it was getting too late to phone people."

"No problem. Are you aware that his family gave me hell?"

"I know, I know! They asked me questions about you and I explained to them that not only did you protect their relative from aspiration pneumonia, but you probably saved his life."

"His laryngospasm saved him from aspiration pneumonia, Jay. I only allowed him to breathe again. Is the family still mad at me?"

"Are you kidding? Now that they understand exactly what went on in the recovery room and, they are grateful to you and sorry for their behavior. They will probably apologize to you when they see you. The entire clan is with the patient upstairs. He's in a private room."

"The family is there? Screw them! You have no idea how they insulted me! Let them send their apologies by mail. And ask them to write it on toilet paper. I have a good place for their words of sorrow. A place where the sun doesn't shine. I don't want to see them again. If Mr. Kennedy is fine, I'm going directly to the OR I start at 7:00."

"I'll join you, Phil. I'm going there, too. My first case is a hernia repair. Yours?"

"A jaw wiring."

"Nasal intubation?"

"Yes. Jacobson asked for one."

They took the down elevator together.

twenty-eight

When both, the upper and the lower jawbones are fractured, the anesthesiologist has a problem. At the end of the operation, after the maxilla and the mandible are individually fixated with wires, the oral surgeon immobilizes the mandible by attaching its wires, with the help of strong rubber bands, to the wires of the upper jaw. The mouth is now totally closed and immobile, while the patient has to still be kept asleep and ventilated. Where is the problem? The problem is maintaining an adequate airway.

In most other operations needing tracheal intubation, the tube is introduced through the mouth. But not in fractured jawbones cases. In such cases, the mouth has to be left completely available to the surgeon and the anesthesiologist has to be able to breathe for the patient throughout the case, until the final fracture immobilization takes place.

The introduction of a breathing tube through the nose into the windpipe is a difficult, but necessary, procedure. The nasal passages are small and prone to bleeding. Therefore, the tube is of a much smaller diameter than the oro-tracheal tube indicated in a similar size patient. In very rare cases, after repeated unsuccessful naso-tracheal intubation attempts, tracheotomies become imperative.

Resting horizontally on his back, head on a pillow, the patient appeared calm. The pre-op medication ordered by the anesthesiologist on call was taking effect. After checking all the medical notes on Joseph Murphy's chart and checking to see if the name matched the *consent for surgery* signature, Newman introduced himself to the wounded biker. Philip knew that the anesthesiologist on call probably explained everything the night before, but just to be sure, he always preferred to offer his own explanations on the necessity for general anesthesia, the monitoring devices, the airway dilemma and the obligatory passing of breathing tube through the nose. He wanted to be sure that the patient knew that this may cause nasal pains after the operation and epistaxis or nosebleed. He ended mentioning the slight possibility of the need for a *tracheotomy*.

"What's that, Doc?"

"You know, an opening in your neck, a tube sticking out of your windpipe, like, what was his name, the *Superman* actor had, after he fell off his horse….."

"Christopher Reeve?"

"Yes, him. But his tracheotomy was permanent. If you do end up needing one, yours will only be temporary. Do you understand me, Mr. Murphy?"

"Yes, Doc. Go ahead. I can take it!"

After Philip made sure that the Afrin was sprayed inside both nasal canals, he asked the patient to blow repeatedly through his nose, while his skilled and gloved finger pinched the lower side of each nostril. The right side seemed to be exchanging more air. This is where, after the induction of anesthesia, the tube will go.

Dr. Jacobson made his appearance, followed by a second, younger man.

"Good morning, Phil! Have you met my new assisting partner, Dr. Rahman? His real first name is Saleem, but we call him Sam."

"Good morning Sandy and good morning, Sam. My real name is Doctor Philip Newman but, after we work together for at least five minutes, you can call me Phil."

"Good morning, Dr. Newman. Nice to know you."

The polite Dr. Saleem Rahman spoke with a British accent. This made Newman curious. "Where are you from Sam?"

"I was born in Manchester, England. My family comes from Pakistan."

Jacobson interrupted, "Are we ready, Phil? You'll have plenty of time to know each other during the operation. It will be a long case."

"Ready to start Sandy. I'm ready and Mr. Murphy is ready, too. Just say hello to your patient and go wash your hands."

Both oral surgeons shook Joseph Murphy's right hand and left the room.

The induction of general anesthesia was uneventful. As expected, the naso-tracheal intubation was a bit tricky, but routine. After paralyzing the anesthetized patient, Philip carefully pushed the well lubricated breathing pipe through the right nostril, until the moment he felt the frictional resistance easing. The cuffed tip of the tube was now in the pharynx.

With Nora, the well trained circulating nurse standing on his right side ready to help, Newman opened the patient's mouth and, with his left hand, introduced the lit laryngoscope. As soon as he was able to visually locate the end of the tube sticking out of the posterior nasal canal, Phil took an angled clamp in his right hand, and, while Nora gingerly pushed on the tube right nostril tube, he grabbed the other end of the tube with the clamp and carefully guided it through the larynx into the trachea. As soon as the deflated cuff passed the level of the vocal cords, Philip asked Nora to stop pushing. The naso-tracheal tube was in place.

With both the laryngoscope and the clamp now safely placed on the dirty tray, the anesthesiologist inflated the cuff with the air syringe. There were no apparent leaks. The lungs were equally ventilated. Satisfied, Newman used narrow adhesive tape to secure the tube to the nose, cheeks and the forehead of the sleeping patient and, for added protection, he applied an ophthalmic ointment inside the eyes and taped the upper lids down.

As soon as the scrubbed surgeons returned with their dripping hands up in the air, they were quickly towel-dried, gowned and gloved. The three hour surgical procedure started exactly at 7 o'clock in the morning and Sanford Jacobson was right. Phil and Sam had plenty of time to chat. Plenty of time for Philip Newman to learn lots of interesting things..

twenty-nine

Newman's restlessness was growing with each passing minute. He was now eager to see his workday come to an end, eager to go home, eager to discuss his new theory with Mike Rooney: *Islamic terror in the OR.*

After all, everybody knew that Afghanistan meant Taliban, Taliban meant Al-Qaeda and Al-Qaeda meant young, brainwashed and stupid young volunteers, ready to fight, ready to die for the cause. Was this the answer they were looking for?

But he had to be patient. The repair of the fractured jaw took half an hour longer than scheduled. By the end of the case, Philip was able to regain his cool. Just another working anesthesia day in a suburban operating room. As soon as the wiring was done and the lower jaw attached to the upper, Phil carefully deflated the cuff inside the windpipe and slowly removed the nasotracheal tube. He replaced it with a softer, shorter, nasal airway, better tolerated by the awakening patient and much better appreciated by the recovery room nurses. There was no obvious bleeding in the right nostril.

By the time Philip returned to the post anesthesia care unit with his next patient, Joseph Murphy was already sitting up in his bed, breathing through a humidified oxygen mask attached to his face by elastic bands circling his head. When asked by Newman how he felt, Murphy only complained in a hoarse voice of "a little bit of pain."

The anesthesiologist lifted the green plastic mask from the patient's face high enough to allow the removal of the nasal tube. After allowing the mask to slowly be pulled back in place by the elastics, he said, "You did great, Mr. Murphy! Ready for some pain medications?"

"Thank you, Doc! The nurse just gave me a shot. I hope it will start to work soon."

"It will, it will, Joe. It always does."

The next two operations were also oral surgery cases but the general anesthesia involved was easier. No nasal intubation necessary for dental extractions. Routine oro-tracheal was enough for the removal of impacted wisdom teeth. By the time Philip Newman MD pulled into his garage, the fractured jaw patient was back in his regular hospital bed. The dental extraction patients were getting ready to be driven home, plastic ice bags on their swollen cheeks, pain medications and antibiotics tablets inside paper bags. The analgesic was to be taken every four hours, as necessary.

After quickly checking his answering machine and his email, Phil dialed the Los Angeles anesthesiologist on his speed dial. It only rang two times before a male voice answered, "Dr. Rooney speaking..."

"Hi, Mike! Phil Newman here."

"Hi, Phil! What's new?"

"I apologize for not answering you sooner, Mike, but I had nothing new to tell you. Until now. It came to me this morning when I met a British surgeon of Pakistani origin. It has something to do with the last message you left on my answering machine. It is possible that we are on the wrong trail. Try to guess."

"Please explain. Don't keep me in suspense."

"You remember the story of the kid who asked to be vaccinated for Encephalitis, Hepatitis and other stuff before he took the trip from which he came back tattooed?"

"Of course, I remember. He was the subject of my last message."

"Exactly. Do you know why he asked for such inoculations?"

"To be safe during his travel?"

"I don't think that he really cared about his safety or his health, Mike. The truth is that without such vaccinations, our authorities don't let you travel to the Indian sub-continent."

"The Indian sub-continent? What are you talking about?"

"India, Pakistan, Afghanistan and three or four other countries. It means that it is possible that after their vaccinations, our young men went to Afghanistan like the other young American did. What was his name? Ah, yes: John Walker. It means that we could be dealing with young people indoctrinated by fanatical Taliban or Al Qaeda followers. Young, brainwashed homegrown terrorists, men and women, ready to fight, ready to die for the cause."

"People die for their cause in their own countries Phil. Not on American OR tables."

"Don't be so sure, Mike. Those fanatic kids commit suicide in Jerusalem, Tel-Aviv, Baghdad, Kabul, Bali, Taba and even in London, England. Why? Just to slaughter innocent people. Why shouldn't they kill themselves under anesthesia in the United States to collect money for their cause? Terrorists need money, Mike. Lots of money! With Sadam Hussein dead and the Al Qaeda's bank accounts frozen, where is their cash coming from? I don't know if you read on the west coast the news about the FBI raid at a mosque in Albany, New York. It happened during the summer of 2004 I think. Apparently, the Imams there were raising money for the Islamic fighters. And they got caught. The insurgents are ingenious people. They have to continuously come up with new, creative and less detectable money raising methods. And I think they did. At our expense."

"The medical malpractice settlements?"

"Exactly! The money from the lawsuits plus the money from the term life insurance policies. A million in New York, another million in Los Angeles and God only knows how much money obtained from San Francisco, Detroit and other cities. We are a big, rich country, Mike. A big country with a stinking legal system. A country in which, a comedian once said, *"99% of lawyers give the others a bad name."* I don't know for sure, of course, if attorneys are directly involved. The lawyers always know where the money is coming from, but I don't think they know each and every time where the money is going. And even if they knew, I am convinced they wouldn't care. The *ambulance chasers* take one third of the booty and ask no questions. But the terrorists know everything about our American medical system. They know that if they stagger the hospitals where suicides occur, they could continue doing this forever. Our hospital administrators and its doctors won't put two and two together. Why waste time trying to explain the cause of an OR. death in the absence of an autopsy? Too complicated! Too time consuming! Most doctors spend their free time playing golf, not solving mysteries."

"Wow, this is incredible! It really makes sense Phil. None of the next-of-kins of our *Code Blues* cases gave permission for an autopsy. As far as I can see, the Islamic religion seems to allow decapitations, while they consider post-mortem examinations a desecration of the human body. But, why the tattoos?"

"Why the tattoos? Very simple. The kids get tattoos, so they can have a reason to have them removed under anesthesia. It is a sure way to end up needing surgery. Not everybody is a proud owner of a hernia to be fixed or of a cyst to be excised. Terrorists seem to have common links, Mike. In Israel, they wear explosive belts, in Iraq they drive car-bombs and, if you remember, most of the hijackers who committed suicide on September 11, also had one thing in common: they took flying lessons. They were not curious to learn how to take-off or how to land. Their interest was flying. Just flying. And our flight schools complied, without asking questions."

After Newman coughed to clear his voice, he continued:

"The majority of our self-immolators also have one thing in common: they were all scheduled for the surgical removal of tattoos under anesthesia. Of course, not every terrorist comes to an American hospital for a tattoo removal and not every tattoo removal candidate is a terrorist. But it is up to us to be vigilant. We must stop the destruction of our profession by these Islamic desperadoes."

"Very, very interesting Phil. I think you're 100 percent right. And me with my stupid toxic tattoo ink theory…"

"Don't say that, Mike. Your theory is a good one. So are the Ephedra, the drug interaction and the allergy possibilities. But they only try to solve the mystery of infrequent occurrences. Of individual cases. Just like when I thought that my deceased young man was a helpless cancer patient who committed suicide, hoping to leave money for his family. But as you can see, all our theories put together don't explain the mass refusal of post-mortem examinations. Do you think that your private detective could find out how many of these unexplained cardiac-arrest patients had direct ties to the Islamic movement? How many of the dead young people had converted to Islam?"

Mike Rooney remained silent for a short moment. Then Newman heard the noise of a squeaking chair followed by the sound of paper shuffling. Rooney resumed, "my private detective? He probably could do that, but I have a better idea. My older brother, Peter, is a big shot at the FBI. I don't know exactly what his responsibilities are – he never talks about what he does – but I do know that he was recently transferred temporarily to the department of Homeland Security. I'm just looking for his phone number. If your theory is correct, and I think it is, we are facing a national rather than a local problem. A private detective will not be enough to solve our enigma, to clarify the jigsaw puzzle. I will talk to my brother as soon as I can. I'll explain our situation and get his opinion. The problem is that he is often out of the country. Peter seems to travel a lot. God knows where he is at this moment, but as soon as I get a hold of him, I will let you know. I will give you a blow by blow description of the conversation I had with him. Okay, Phil?"

"It sounds great. I'm looking forward to hearing from you."

thirty

It may sound paradoxical, but his alarming theory that the sudden epidemic of unexpected cardiac arrests under anesthesia had been executed by young fanatics eager to raise money for their cause, did not scare Philip Newman. On the contrary, he felt relieved. If all this was true, then the death of James Walker was no longer his fault. No longer a medical malpractice   case. Rather than being faced with a rash of operating room mistakes all around the country, they were now confronted by a new kind of global menace: terrorism in the operating room. Suddenly, the irony struck Phil. "Terror in the OR.?...and why not?" he muttered to himself, "The word *TerrOR* does end in *OR!*"

He felt reassured and burned out at the same time. Tired of worrying about the professional, mental and financial consequences of the lawsuit. All of a sudden, Phil felt drained from dealing with difficult to manage patients and with their next-of-kin. And to top it all, he was dreading being on call for the entire upcoming weekend. But he was. He needed a break, some precious time off. It was time to go away on a short but necessary vacation. After all, in today's modern world, it's easy to keep abreast of developing events by Internet or phone, no matter where you are..

He glanced at the calendar. It was the middle of October. The next annual American Society of Anesthesiologists meeting was starting on Saturday in two weeks, at the Sixth Avenue Hilton, in Manhattan. Ed Morris would probably be happy to let him go. Nobody from the group was planning a vacation that week. If Kyra could take some time-off at the same time, he would book a room at the Hilton starting the Tuesday before, so they could spend some time together rediscovering the City of New York.

During the five day meeting, he would meet Mike Rooney and some of the other contributors to the *UNEXPECTED DEATH UNDER ANESTHESIA* web page. And while he was busy with the convention, Kyra could go to museums, do some shopping and have lunch with a few of her old girlfriends. It would be great. He could spend some much needed time with his beautiful wife while on a tax-deductible business trip.

Just to be 100% sure, Newman called his chief. "Two weeks off? No problem, Phil" was the immediate answer. "I'll write it down right away, so I won't forget. I'm starting to forget things, you know."

Phil did not plan to depart before Tuesday. A demonstration of the *Bispectral Index Monitor* was scheduled for that Monday in the *Soundedge Hospital Medical Library* at 4 o'clock in the afternoon. It was important that he attends. If the system worked the way its manufacturer was claiming, it would represent an important new monitoring system. The *BIS* was supposed to prevent *awareness while under anesthesia.*

So far, he had never had such a problem in his practice. Not even once. But more and more cases of awareness were being reported in the media. It must be a horrible feeling to find oneself paralyzed by drugs and partially awake while the surgeons are cutting. The classic reliance on vital signs such as heart rate and blood pressure and the use of standard dosages to ensure that the patient received adequate levels of anesthetic was no longer enough. With rampant substance abuse, people are becoming more and more resistant to narcotics. It was impossible to determine in advance a patient's resistance to such medications. He tried for a while to monitor the depth of his general anesthetics with an EEG machine but, in the end, he found the electroencephalographic monitoring complicated, distracting and time consuming. His attendance to the *BIS* meeting was a must.

When Kyra came home from work, Philip greeted her with a big kiss. Unexpectedly, the routine kiss lead to a passionate one, a local caress became generalized and, without any advance planning, they made love. It was fantastic! Spontaneous and unexpected love making in a married couple? This hasn't happened in ages!

When Phil brought up, during supper, the subject of a NYC vacation and asked Kyra if she could take the next two weeks off, she quickly left the room to make the arrangements. Excited, Kyra returned with the phone in her hand. "Phil, I got the time off. It will be great to take a vacation, just the two of us!"

As soon as he finished eating, Philip called the 24 hour Hilton Reservations line to make sure there were still rooms available. There were only a few left for the physicians participating in the convention. A nine day booking in the name of *Dr. Newman and company* was immediately made.

T he Saturday and Sunday calls were exhausting. Newman could not remember a busier weekend, ever. Was this just the luck of the draw or was Port Lincoln experiencing an explosive growth? Two appendectomies, one traumatic splenectomy, four cesarean sections, three fractured hips, a couple of incomplete abortions and a change of cardiac pacemaker. On top of that, there were the Saturday morning post-op visits and the Sunday evening pre-op consultations, on all the patients admitted for Monday surgery. During those forty-eight hours he must have slept a total of three and half hours!

An anesthesiologist, like any human being, never really gets used to the lack of sleep. But follow such an acute lack of sleep with an eight uninterrupted hours of total repose and the same anesthesiologist will wake up completely rested and reinvigorated. It doesn't matter how many non-stop hours he worked before the therapeutic and reparative slumber.

Philip Newman returned home at 6:30 Monday morning. After a light breakfast without coffee, he went to bed at 7:00. Kyra made sure that the ringer on the bedroom phone was off and the window shades closed. On her first day of vacation, she was going to quietly take care of the house. Dust and rearrange the furniture etc. No vacuum cleaners, no hair dryers. Making noises was a no-no when married to an anesthesiologist recovering from a week-end call.

Before going to sleep, Phil changed the alarm setting on his bedside clock to 3 o'clock in the afternoon. He needed an entire hour to shower, shave and grab some lunch before attending the 4 PM BIS meeting. But Dr. Newman woke up, as usual, five minutes before the alarm rang. He arrived at the Soundedge Hospital library at 3:55.

The Bispectral seminar started with an interesting demonstration. The demonstrator explained that, rather than trying to guess the individual needs of each patient, the modern anesthesiologist finally has at his disposal the use of a sensor strip. The sensor strip is placed, during surgery, on the anesthetized person's forehead and it records brain activity. The results are sent to the monitor, which computes a number ranging from zero to one hundred. In a well calibrated machine, this number was supposed to correlate with the patient's level of consciousness. A reading of 100 meant that the patient is wide awake. Under 60, likely to be unconscious. Phil smiled to himself, wondering what would happen it he could attach the sensor strip to the forehead of some of the operating surgeons? How many will compute 100?

According to the salesman, the clinical studies of the BIS monitor had shown that customizing anesthesia levels to patient's needs can help them wake up faster and feel alert sooner. On top of it, they experienced fewer side effects such as muscle aches, nausea and vomiting. The device also promised to minimize the risk of lawsuits caused by *intraoperative awareness* cases.

In Newman's opinion, the pushy manufacturer's rep. went overboard during his presentation. He made it sound like, "If you buy our expensive BIS monitor and attach your patient to it, your worries are over!" An experienced doctor knows that such a device does not exist. Nothing is 100% sure. After all, even the BIS demonstrator did not dare to use the phrase *eliminates the risks*. He only used the word *minimize*.

A physician should always base final decisions on his professional judgment. No machine could replace a doctor's sagacity. Monitoring devices should never substitute for medical experience.

Newman went home informed, but not totally convinced. He was leery of "clinical studies." Hadn't Phen-Phen and Vioxx passed satisfactory clinical studies before the ill-fated pills were allowed to flood the market? And how about all those recalled breast implants, heart valves and cardiac pacemakers, to name just a few?

Phil stopped his car at the entrance of his driveway and pushed the garage opener button. The stupid gadget did not work. Another electronic device ready to be recalled? He parked the car outside and walked toward the front porch. Kyra was waiting in the open door. "How was the meeting, Phil?" She put her arms around his neck and kissed him on the lips.

"The meeting was *verrrry* interesting my love. Another modern electronic gadget which, when least expected, will stop working. Just like our garage opener." He kissed her back.

"The garage opener works too well! The door opened all by itself today, while you were away. I don't know why. A car was stopped at the time in front of our house. Is it possible that by coincidence, a stranger has the same garage door opener code as ours? Or is this a new way to break in to people's homes? All I know is that the car left when they saw me entering the garage. You were not able to open the garage because I pushed on the security button to prevent the opening of the door by remote."

"It is somehow possible, Kyra, for two different openers to have the same codes but, why would anyone push on his garage opener away from his own house? In front of someone else's garage? This is fishy. If we still have the brochure for the opener, I will try to change the security code myself. If not, let's call a technician. OK?"

"OK, Phil." They entered the front hallway together. Philip closed and locked the door behind them.

"Anything else happened during my absence?""

"Let's see…yes. Dr. Rooney called from Los Angeles. He said that he spoke to his brother and would like you to call him back at home. He left his home phone number."

"I already have his number. Did he, by any chance, mention what his brother thought about my ideas?"

"Yes, he did. His brother thinks that you may be right."

"Thank you, Kyra! I love you." He kissed her with passion.

thirty-two

Seconds after Philip finished dialing from his home in Long Island, the phone started ringing in Los Angeles. It only rang twice. "Dr. Rooney speaking..."

"Good afternoon, Mike. This is Newman from New York."

"Like I didn't know. I was waiting for your call Phil. Exciting things are happening."

"I know. My wife gave me the news. Apparently your brother smells a rat too. Does he plan to get involved?"

"And how! Peter will come to the Hilton on Tuesday to meet with us and discuss the mode of action. I'm arriving on Friday, the day before the meeting. My wife is coming, too. What are your plans?"

"Both Kyra and I are on vacation. We are leaving for the Big Apple tomorrow morning."

"Good for you. Enjoy! October in New York must be nice. By the way Phil, Peter already got in contact with some of the anesthesiologists enlisted on our website and was able to obtain a few names and social security numbers from their hospital charts. At this moment, he is investigating some of the lives of the deceased young patients: their birth locations, social behaviors, memberships, travel, vaccination histories and even, whenever possible, their emails. My brother is not fooling around. He seems inspired by the attacks on the Spanish trains and the bombing in London by their home-grown suicidal terrorists. You probably remember the events. As soon as Peter makes a decision, he doesn't waste time."

"Great, Mike! Who knows? Maybe we can solve those unexplainable cardiac arrests, eliminate some of the medical malpractice lawsuits and lower our professional liability insurance rates for a change."

"Keep on dreaming, Phil!" Rooney answered in a laughing voice. "See you at the convention. We are booked at the Hilton. Are you staying there, too?"

"Yes. I prefer to be on site. We will do enough walking in the city as it is. We are coming in by train."

"I agree. It's nice to take a break from the daily driving. See you soon, Dr. Newman."

"Good-bye, Dr. Rooney."

Their suitcases were ready. When it came to preparations for travel, Kyra did not trust her husband. She did all the packing. Now all they had to do next morning, was to have breakfast and call a taxi. The distance from their house to the train station was only two miles. They watched the 11 o'clock news and the beginning of *The Tonight Show*. It felt good being on vacation, nice to go to bed late for a change and not worrying about being tired the next day.

Newman was in a deep sleep when the phone rang. His interlocutor recognized that immediately. "How come you're still asleep, Phil? We are waiting for you here!" Philip didn't recognize the voice. He hated when people did not introduce themselves. It must be a surgeon, he thought. surgeons always think that they are the most important people on earth; convinced that everybody should recognize their voices. He got up and sat at the edge of the bed.

"Who's there?"

"It's me, Phil. Ron! Ron Stevenson. You have a request in my room. My 7:30 cataract patient wants you and only you. Didn't they tell you? My office gave this information to the OR secretary four weeks ago, when the case was booked!"

"Nobody told me anything! What time is it now, Ron?"

"7:15. I can't change my cases around. My second patient wasn't admitted yet. Are you coming, Phil?"

"I'll be there in about twenty five minutes."

"Thanks! We'll have everything ready. See you soon."

Awaken by the phone call, Kyra was already up. "Did they schedule you for a case, Phil? Don't they know you're on vacation? Do you want some breakfast?"

"Don't bother, Kyra. It's just a cataract request that I was not informed about. Somebody screwed up. I'll eat and shave when I come back. We'll just have to leave a couple of hours later than planned, that's all."

After a quick shower, he got dressed and left. There was no point on trying to investigate the scheduling screw up. Either Stevenson's office forgot to inform the Soundedge OR, or the OR secretary forgot to tell him. Tracking down the culprit would be futile.

Preparing for just one case didn't take long. The anesthesia started at 5 minutes before 8:00.

Ron Stevenson was a dinosaur among ophthalmologists. The old-timer should have retired four or five years ago, but chose to continue working. Why wouldn't he retire? Fear of idleness? Money woes? Plain greed? Who knows? For sure it wasn't his love for the profession. He practiced his eye surgery the old fashioned way. No point to waste time by keeping up with medical innovations. After all, he was as busy as ever using the same methods he had used for the past thirty years. His patients didn't know there was a difference. They had no idea that the younger eye surgeons, using newer methods, were extracting cataracts faster, better, with less pain and with similar, if not better, results.

Cataracts are rarely a juvenile problem. As a rule, older patients prefer to be under the care of an older eye doctor, under the false belief that *older* meant *more experienced* and *more experienced* meant *better.* This was certainly not always true but, it was not up to Philip Newman to tell such cataract patients that they were misinformed. If nobody asks for advice, it is better to keep opinions to himself.

The operation went well. As soon as he provided the monitored patient with sufficient oxygen through a nasal cannula, Philip put him in deep intravenous sedation, for the duration of the *retro-bulbar block.* Stevenson was now the only Soundedge ophthalmologist still using this very painful, behind the eye injection, allowing him to perform the surgery. In the newer and faster *phacoemulsification* techniques, the numbing was obtained by a simpler *topical* anesthetic: a few drops of local anesthetic repeatedly dripped in the eye. The operation was performed through a smaller and less painful ultrasound or laser probe incision. A much lighter form of anesthetic sedation was needed and the patient went home faster, less groggy, and with less chances of getting sick afterwards.

After leaving his awakening patient in the post anesthesia care unit, Newman took advantage of his unexpected presence in the hospital and went upstairs to revisit all the patients he had anesthetized during the weekend. They were all doing as well as expected. Before returning home to finally start his vacation, he stopped by the recovery room again. The cataract patient was being discharged. He thanked Phil while they shook hands.

Kyra was waiting in the dining room, with a delicious breakfast. They ate and after the meal, he showered while she called for a taxi. They were now ready for the TPV. *TPV* was the nickname Philip gave the Long Island Railroad after they returned from a vacation in Paris. During this trip, the Newmans used French public transportation and they were very much impressed by the *TGV* or *Tres Grande* Vitesse meaning :*Very Great Speed*, the official name given to the French high-speed rail transportation. Comparatively, the LIRR train was a snail-paced *TPV* or *Tres Petite Vitesse* meaning *Very Little Speed.*

The classic Long Island Railroad joke was the printed sign somebody hung inside the Port Lincoln station: "IT IS FORBIDDEN TO PICK FLOWERS WHILE THE TRAIN IS MOVING."

But the Newmans still preferred the relaxed travel in a slow train, to the bumper to bumper car traffic on the ironically named Long Island Expressway. If you have to deal with traffic delays into Manhattan, at least in the train, you are able to read a book or the newspapers, while you travel. The 11:15 train left Port Lincoln at 11:18 and arrived at Pennsylvania Station in Manhattan at 13:21. Outside, on Seventh Avenue, the yellow cabs were waiting in line. Kyra and Philip grabbed the first taxi and, 45 minutes later, they were already hanging their clothes in the large closet of their *room with a view.* The Sixth Avenue Hilton was a sophisticated hotel. Twenty Eight floors down below, New York City was waiting.

thirty-three

For Kyra, the location of the Manhattan Hilton on West 53rd Street and Sixth Avenue was ideal. So many of New York's cultural treasures were within walking distance. She could easily catch an exhibit at the Museum of Modern Art if not a concert at Carnegie Hall or Lincoln Center. Central Park was a stroll away. Broadway? Just around the corner. Of course, great shopping was no further than one block away on Fifth Avenue.

For Philip, the hotel's proximity to these cultural Meccas was less important. He valued the Hilton because it was three blocks away from the Carnegie Deli. Phil adored this kosher restaurant with its delicious jars of pickles on every table. Customers crunched away as they pondered selections from the copious menu. He had to eat there at least once during each Manhattan visit.

It was now past 2 o'clock in the afternoon and Phil was beginning to feel hungry. Could there be a better place to start a New York City vacation than at the famous Deli on West 55th Street and 7th Avenue? The *Broadway Danny Rose* (appellation given to one of the best pastrami and corned beef sandwiches in New York) was calling his name.

For Kyra, this was her first Carnegie Deli visit and she really enjoyed the unique ambiance of the noisy, bustling restaurant. Perusing the extensive menu of sandwiches named for famous living and no longer living clients, Kyra turned to Phil, "Who knows, my love? Maybe one day they will have your favorite sandwich on their menu too. The *Dr. Philip Newman's Ham and Camembert with Horseradish Sauce on Rye Bread, Double-Decker.*"

Philip started laughing. "ham in a kosher Jewish deli?"

Kyra put her right hand over her mouth. "Oops! I forgot!"

Philip moved toward her just far enough for a kiss on her cheek. "You know what, my sweetie? You just used an expression I haven't heard in years! A word which is not allowed in operating rooms. Probably banned by the American College of Surgeons!"

"Are you serious, Phil? Are they really allowed to ban expressions? Is this possible? Which one is the forbidden word?"

"Do I have to explain everything to you, Kyra? My God! How innocent those pediatric nurses are! The absolute taboo surgical word is: *OOPS!*"

She started laughing. "Thank God, I begin to see that my old husband is back. When Philip starts telling corny jokes, it means Philip is feeling better! You have no idea how much I've suffered waiting for my real husband to re-emerge."

"I know, I know. I was totally aware of the effects of this deep depression on you, but, I couldn't help it, Kyra. The OR death and the malpractice lawsuit, temporarily destroyed me."

"It destroyed both of us Philip. But I knew we could get through it. The for better or worse bit." After a short pause, Kyra continued, "I have to tell you something, Phil. Are you ready?"

"Go ahead, sweetheart."

"You know how when you were depressed, we stopped making love?"

"Of course, Kyra. My mind was somewhere else. And?"

"Well, after a while I stopped taking my birth control medication. I was starting to have some unpleasant side effects from it and made an appointment to see my OB-GYN. Therefore, the other day, when we unexpectedly had sex, I was no longer on the pill."

"But, Kyra? What about Tay-Sachs? You know about my late son, Jacob. I couldn't go through that again."

"Phil, I'm not trying to get pregnant! But if it was to happen, there would be no risk of Tay-Sachs. My Doctor screened me for it a few years ago and confirmed I was not a carrier. You need two carriers to pass on Tay-Sachs disease."

Phil sat stunned. "Kyra, do you want to have a baby?"

As Kyra answered, her eyes welled up. "Yes, Phil. Nothing would make me happier."

After a long interval of silence, Phil spoke deliberately. "I have been so selfish. I never considered your feelings. I want you to be happy, my love. We should try to have a baby. From now on, you are a potential future mother!"

Not being able to contain her elation, Kyra started laughing. With total disregard for the people around, Philip kissed her with passion.

Their vacation started on a good note. They filled their days of freedom before the convention with walks in Central Park, site-seeing, *The Lion King* on Broadway, and shopping. In between there were museum visits, art galleries and romantic dinners. They started each day with breakfast and love making in their hotel room. The only time they had a real lunch in a restaurant was the first day, at the Carnegie Deli. They soon realized that if you want to enjoy your dinner, you have to skip lunch. A hot dog in the street was enough. And the New York City franks were the best.

thirty-four

Friday started like all their other mornings at the Hilton: making love. Those few days at the hotel were totally rejuvenating. The Newmans found themselves more sexually active than during their honeymoon. And, for some unknown reason, on the last day before the convention their libidos were even more intense. After a late continental breakfast of cappuccino and croissant at a nearby Starbucks and after a walk in Central Park, they decided to return to their room and rest a little. Not only had they have walked enough for the last few days but, now, the skies were getting dark and cloudy. With torrential rains appearing imminent, they returned immediately to the Hilton. The room was already cleaned and the bed made. After posting the *DO NOT DISTURB* sign on their door, they went to lie down for a rest but, to no avail. Instead of resting, they made love again. It was fantastic! Why is sex always more exciting in a hotel room than in the privacy of your own home?

They were in a blissful post-coital trance when the phone rang. Philip picked up the receiver and said "Hello," in a sleepy voice.

"Hi, Phil, it's Mike Rooney. It sounds to me like I woke you up. Sorry!"

"No problem, Mike. Just a catnap. Are you in the hotel?"

"Yes. We arrived half an hour ago. Do you have any plans for supper?"

"Not yet. You?"

"We would like to eat at the hotel. We're a little tired. Don't forget that, in addition to the hours we spent traveling, we are also now three hours older than we were in Los Angeles."

Philip started laughing. "But you'll be three hours younger when you go back to California. Dining in the hotel? Great idea! 8 o'clock?"

"How about 7:30? I would like to go to bed early and avoid falling asleep during lectures tomorrow."

"Yes. You're right, Mike. Anesthetic lectures can put people to sleep! OK 7.30, it is. I'll make a reservation for four. See you in the restaurant."

"Great, Phil. We'll be on time!"

In her supine position, Kyra pushed away her blanket and, still naked, stretched inside the bed. "Honey, what's Mrs. Rooney's first name?"

On his way to the bathroom, Philip stopped and scratched his head. "Mike's wife's name? Good question. I have no idea. I don't think I ever knew her name. We'll find out tonight. Could you please call the hotel restaurant and make a reservation for 7:30, Kyra?"

"No problem, Phil. It'll be great to eat in the hotel. Not a nice night to walk around in Manhattan."

They spent the rest of the afternoon watching a pay-per-view movie in their room. She opened a small bottle of wine from the mini-bar, he drank a beer. Outside, the rain was now non-stop. A few minutes before 7:00 they showered together, washing each other's back.

Elegant, but casually dressed, Kyra and Phil reached the restaurant at the pre-arranged time. A well-dressed couple was standing in front of the maitre d'hotel's desk. Next to the dark-haired man, who seemed to be working hard to disguise a receding hairline, was a striking blond. Both were tall and middle-aged, but well preserved. Philip was the first to speak, "The Rooneys, I presume?"

With a big smile on his face, Mike Rooney extended his right hand toward the arriving duo, "Your presumption is correct, Doctor Newman. If I remember well your beautiful wife's name is Kyra. May I introduce to you to Rita, my better half?"

Philip couldn't help but comment. "Rita Rooney? Very musical name. Nice to finally meet you both!" They shook hands. After informing them that their table was ready, the maitre d' asked if they were ready to be seated. They were. During the short walk to the reserved table, the two ladies made small talk about October weather in New York. Phil and Mike followed quietly.

Kyra sat across from Rita at the elegant square table. The sommelier arrived within seconds. Philip Newman announced his preference for beer. Mike Rooney, the wine connoisseur from Los Angeles, took charge. With both women ordering seafood, he inspected the entire white wine list and ordered a bottle of 1999 Sauvignon Blanc with three wine glasses.

The conversation was fluent. They avoided discussing the cardiac arrest cases. They knew that there would be plenty of time to get into that later when they met with Peter Rooney, the FBI agent and brother. The dialogue remained social. Rita was also a registered nurse. Their discussion concentrated on how they met, how they fell in love, why they chose the medical and the nursing professions and why the two men chose to specialize in Anesthesiology.

Dr. Rooney was an amusing fellow. His personal history was pretty comical. First he tried *emergency room medicine* but, after spending half of his time lancing abscesses and boils, he decided that being *Sir Lance-a-lot* was not for him. He then decided to switch to a surgical residency but was not at all impressed with the casual instructions he received there either. It was in one of those teaching hospitals famous for their *see one, do one, teach one,* learn-as-you-can methods. But in that same hospital, the Anesthesiology department was very impressive. Lead by a Hungarian-born chief of anesthesia, they had regular theoretical and practical classes in their own classroom, their own medical library and a group of fantastic attendings on the staff. The anesthesia residents were always supervised. Even at 2:00 o'clock in the morning.

The food finally arrived. It was better tasting than one expects in a hotel restaurant. The four of them skipped the dessert. Vanity prevailed. The Rooneys ended their supper with decaf, the Newmans with regular espresso. After the coffee, the men informed their wives that, in the morning, they were on their own. The doctors had a group breakfast at the convention.

Kyra and Rita decided to meet at 10 o'clock next morning in the lobby. When the check arrived, they split the tab, adding tips and writing their room numbers above their signatures. Now Mike and Rita apologized for their early departure, explaining that they were eager to go to bed. Kyra and Phil decided to linger for a while.

As soon as they were alone, Philip caressed his wife's hand on the table, "Did you notice their foreheads, baby? Not a wrinkle, not a movement, no expression. Those Californians are surely addicted to Botox!"

Kyra smiled. "Don't worry, honey. The New Yorkers are not far behind."

They decided to have an after dinner drink. Drambuie for her, Benedictine and Brandy for him. He signed the bill and, after finishing their liqueurs, they got up gingerly and walked hand in hand to the elevator. In the room, the bed was already open, still left undone from their afternoon encounter. Both went to sleep fast. They couldn't even dream of making love on a full stomach.

thirty-five

At first glance, this Anesthesiology convention closely resembled a *flea market*. The walls of the main hallway were lined with tables displaying all kinds of gadgets for sale. There were even T-shirts offered on which the anesthesiologist's name would be printed above the design of a laryngoscope and a pen sticking out of a pocket. Of course, the prices were much higher than in a *flea market*. Most of the medical instruments offered for sale were all too familiar to Phil. After all, new revolutionary devices are not invented every day.

Newman liked to review all the manufacturer's stands anyway. He needed reassurance that he was instrumentally and electronically up-to-date. He soon discovered that Rooney liked to do the same. After a copious buffer breakfast, they visited the anesthetic instrumentation gallery and Mike ordered a couple of *The Magill pediatric forceps* to be sent to his hospital. Philip bought nothing. When it came to intubating children, Soundedge had all the instrumentation they needed.

They separated after discussing their Tuesday meeting with Peter Rooney. Phil and Mike chose to attend different lectures. Every time he went to an anesthesia convention, Philip insisted on participating in the *Malignant Hyperthermia* symposium. Once you are involved in such a rare event, you never forget it. It remains a life-time paranoid anesthetic obsession. But other anesthesiologists, the ones who had never faced the Malignant Hyperthermia nightmare, were convinced that the syndrome was totally exaggerated and blown out of proportion. Dr. Rooney shared such belief.

Philip Newman never had such a case himself either but, some years ago, he helped Ed Morris with one. It took many agonizing hours to save the young patient's life. The acute life threatening disorder, better known as MH develops during or after a general anesthetic in people with a genetic predisposition, and only if triggering anesthetic agents are used. In patients with this metabolic disorder, specific – but widely used – general anesthetics cause a potentially fatal increase in carbon dioxide excretion, muscle rigidity and high fever.

The introduction of Dantrolene Sodium changed the entire picture of the MH treatment. Before its 1979 introduction, the MH mortality rate from cardiac arrest, brain damage, or internal hemorrhage was 4 out of 5 patients. The only known treatment available was cooling. Putting the entire body of the patient in ice Dr. Newman learned how to use the Dantrolene the first time the medication was presented at a convention. The results of Dantrolene on the lowering of body temperature and on the improvement on the total muscular rigidity, especially the spasticity of the masseter, were impressive. The masseter, the muscle we bite with, is by far the strongest muscle in the entire body. When an anesthesiologist is not able to open his anesthetized patient's mouth, he never forgets it.

MH was first described in 1960 and it took a good few years before people with the known genetic predisposition began to wear *Medic-Alert* bracelets on their wrists. But there are still plenty of predisposed patients totally unaware and having general anesthesia for the first time.

Recent news analyzed even the possibility of *Malignant Hyperthermia* in some of the people who recently lost their lives receiving a powerful electric jolt, after being shot with a *Taser Gun.*

Reassured that he was up to date on latest MH. news, Newman decided to return to his room for a break. There were no other lectures of interest to him that day. The seminar on *New Developments in Cardiac Pumps* was an important subject, but not pertinent to him. The Soundedge General Hospital was not an open heart surgery center.

The weather outside was improving. Philip walked for a couple of blocks to stretch his legs, before returning to his room. His wife was not there. Kyra was probably fulfilling her passion for museums, perhaps with her new friend, Rita Rooney.

After brushing his teeth, Phil checked his answering machine at home. No messages. He flipped around the channels on the television, but nothing interested him. He switched to the hotel computer to check the stock market and to read his email. One email, waiting amongst all the spam, immediately caught his attention: another unexplainable anesthetic death in Phoenix, Arizona. He checked the *Anesthesiology Web Page* to make sure the case was listed. It was. A nineteen year old man seeking a tattoo removal after returning from a Club Med vacation in Morocco. The events were remarkably similar to his James Walker case. And once again, the post-mortem examination was refused for religious reasons and once again, the medical malpractice lawsuit was filed almost immediately.

Before switching off the computer, he checked the website's calendar. The *To Whom It May Concern* meeting with Peter Rooney was already listed for Tuesday, 4:00 PM. in the lecture room number two, at the Manhattan Hilton. Mike was on the ball.

thirty-six

For Newman and Rooney this annual gathering was different from the two previous ones they attended in Las Vegas and San Francisco. At the Manhattan Hilton, they went only to a few selected lectures. Interested only in the ones absolutely necessary to attend. The most important subject was, as usually, medical liability. Especially the three hours of heated discussion on drug interaction: the arthritic patient who was on Vioxx and suffers a heart attack while under anesthesia. Who should be held responsible? The drug manufacturer or the anesthesiologist? The final answer was not too reassuring for the doctors. It appears that there was no clear-cut medical answer. Only the lawyers knew for sure!

The rest of their convention time was spent on public relations: making as many colleagues as possible aware of the mysterious cardiac arrest epidemic, convince them to become a part of the new web page and inviting them to meet the FBI agent at 4 PM on Tuesday. In the evenings, the two couples had supper in the Hilton restaurant. Accountants are always happier when professional expenses appear on one hotel bill rather than divided between different eating places.

Twenty-seven anesthesiologists were slated to attend Peter Rooney's presentation. Peter Rooney arrived at 20 minutes before four. In a quiet corner of the hotel bar, over a beer, the FBI agent shared some interesting news with his brother and with Newman. A preliminary investigation showed that all the local attorneys involved in the recent medical malpractice suits, belonged to the same nationwide law firm. Peter Rooney discussed the agenda for his presentation and informed them that when the time for the final action will arrive, he would need one of the two anesthesiologists. Philip volunteered without hesitation.

When they entered the lecture room number two, all the 27 anesthesiologists were present. Much better attendance than Phil and Mike have hoped. They all wore, as requested, the picture ID given to them during their convention check-in.

The FBI agent introduced himself briefly and, before starting any other discussions, he checked, one by one, the picture IDs of everybody present without apologizing. Routine security precautions.

Dr. Rooney was the first to speak. He explained the entire situation and the multiple theories behind it. After all, not everybody present had a history of medical malpractice law-suits secondary to unexplainable anesthesia demises. After a quick summary of the events he gave the chair to the FBI representative.

Peter Rooney was laconic but thorough. He emphasized that the FBI agreed only with the terrorist fund-raising theory and will get involved in trying to stop it. The enemy needs money. A recent report even suspects some of the traders in fake designers bags and a few manufacturers of fashion knockoffs, of providing funds to terrorist organizations.

Everything seems possible in our days. In any case, he, or another FBI agent will be present in the company of Dr. Philip Newman during the next suspicious case. The surgical reasons to need anesthesia were sometimes different but, the most common denominator seemed to be the *removal of tattoos with possible skin grafts.* After all, it was God who created hernias, cysts or crooked noses, but never the tattoos. Having their skins engraved, was probably the surest way for suicide candidates in search of a reason, to need and obtain anesthesia.

The FBI. man continued, "We don't know in which of the 50 states the next tattoo removal will take place but, as soon as one such case is booked in your operating room, please let Dr. Philip Newman know. I will be in touch with him at all times. Everybody in favor please lift your right hand." Mike and Philip were the first to raise their hands. The other 27 followed. Peter Rooney chose not to give any further explanations. He said, "good-luck to all of us," and left the room in the company of his brother.

Phil remained behind, to give everybody present his phone numbers. He trusted a phone call better than an info posted on the web.

thirty-seven

The weeks following the Anesthesiology convention, were somewhat of a letdown. After Peter Rooney's motivating presentation, Philip Newman expected that once home, his phone would not stop ringing. No such thing happened. When the telephone did ring, it was just for routine surgical schedule discussions. Did those 27 anesthesiologists who unanimously agreed to cooperate forget their promise? Did the terrorist organizations get wind of the FBI's involvement? Did they stop ordering suicides under anesthesia?

The only unexpected message on the Newman's answering machine came from the medical liability insurance company. The calling agent wanted to inform the good doctor that the James Walker case was already settled out of court. End of message. The effects of the settlement appeared in Newman's mailbox two weeks later: a $12,000 increase in his annual premium. "One more increase like that and...good-bye Anesthesiology!," Phil muttered to himself.

Philip Newman checked the web page and his answering machine several times a day. The year ended with no new *unexplainable demises under anesthesia* being reported.

After a busy New Year's Eve night on call, Phil woke up in the afternoon of January 1st, feeling exhausted. With Mozart playing softly on the stereo, Kyra greeted her husband in the living room, wishing him a Happy New Year. The champagne was chilled and the gas fireplace lit. But Phil was grumpy and not fully awake. He lacked even the energy to brush his teeth. Kyra kissed him on the cheek, then said, "Honey, the Rooney's called while you were asleep to wish us a Happy New Year. Mike wants you to call him back."

Finally some news? Phil took the portable phone from its base. Perhaps he wanted champagne, after all. With the receiver in his right hand, champagne glass in the left, he was still able to press the speed dial button with one finger. After two rings came a voice. "Dr. Rooney speaking."

"Happy New Year, Doctor Mike! What's new in this new year?"

"Happy New Year, Phil! Are you ready for some old year news?"

"Ready, Sir. Shoot!"

"We had an excision of tattoos with skin grafts on December 31st. It was booked at the last minute. The surgeon was going on vacation. I called the Soundedge Hospital but they told me that you were busy doing a case and, on top of it, they told me that you were on call. So I decided not to bother you. After all, not only it was happening in my own hospital and I was the one giving the anesthesia, but my brother happened to be present, too. He and his wife are spending the New Year with us."

"Any problems during the operation?"

"Absolutely none, Phil. It was an extremely calm case. Even the usually spastic plastic surgeon didn't mind waiting an extra hour after we put his patient on the OR table. He didn't have the guts to complain after we allowed him to squeeze his case on the schedule at the last possible moment. Of course we had to invent some technical problems like malfunctioning monitoring machines, to be able to delay the case and ensure that, if the patient went into cardiac arrest, he did that before any anesthetic was administered."

The patient's family was also alarmed by how long the case took, but we assured them that everything was OK. The operation was completed without incident or complications."

"Was Peter disappointed?" Newman queried.

"Not at all. My brother is a true professional. His years in the FBI have taught him the value of waiting. His motto is *'patience, patience and patience again!'* Peter explained to me that a few years ago, he staked out a house for 22 nights in a row before getting his man."

"Why do you think so much time has passed since the last unexplained death? Do you think the terrorists decided to stop committing suicide?"

"No way, my friend! The terrorists need more money today than ever before. Just a quiet period, I presume. They are probably plotting right now where their next suicide should occur. Do you read the *US News & World Report*?"

"No. I only subscribe to *Time Magazine*. What does it say?"

"It was the cover story, quite a while ago. Its title was: *'The New Business of Terror.'* They explain how organized crime is providing the cash that keeps global terrorism going. According to the article, the scams are as varied as the criminal world: drug smuggling and fraud are mainstays, but other activities include car theft, selling pirated CDs, counterfeiting money, etc. etc. One enterprising pair of Jihadists in Germany hoped to fund a suicide mission to Iraq by taking out nearly $1 million in life insurance and staging the death of the insured in a faked traffic accident. Some of the terrorist cells are loosely bound and based on petty crime; others, like the group behind the Madrid bombings, suggest a whole new level of sophistication. US News claims that this bombing which killed 191 Spaniards, cost the terrorists a meager $50,000."

"Wow! Sounds like a well researched and convincing article. Easy cash. Money from life insurance in Germany, money from life insurance and medical liability settlements in the United States. From where I see it, in Germany they hope to get their million. In our country, they get it. When it comes to law-suits against doctors, our jurors give away money like water. By the way, my medical malpractice case was settled out-of-court."

"Out-of-court? Just like the lawyers and the terrorists like it. I bet you have no idea how much they got."

"No, and I'm afraid to ask. All I know is that my insurance premiums went up by one grand a month. We have to stop this nonsense."

"We will, Phil. Happy New Year to you and Kyra!"

"Same to you and Rita. Give her a kiss from us!"

"Consider it done."

After switching off the phone, Philip put the receiver back in its cradle, placed the almost empty champagne glass on the coffee table and went to brush his teeth.

thirty-eight

Philip Newman's assignment on this cold January day was *chest and lungs*. He spent the entire morning and part of the afternoon in operating room five, the *thoracic surgery room,* a surgical alcove morbidly nicknamed *Marlboro Country*. In this OR., known for its abundant sputum and blood, the cleaning and disinfecting between two operations always took longer than in most other rooms.

With time on his hands, Phil decided to check his answering machine after every case. He was thrilled to find a message waiting. It was probably left sometime between the bronchoscopy-biopsy, his second case and the left lower pulmonary lobectomy, his third. The speaker had an accent, possibly Israeli. "Good morning, Doctor Newman. This is Doctor Ethan Rabin from the New Haven Jewish Hospital in Connecticut. We met at the convention and, if you remember, I was a participant in the private meeting. I'm calling to let you know that we have on our elective schedule three weeks from today, a removal of a tattoo with possible skin graft. Please call me at my home, tonight." Philip jotted down the number and put it in his wallet, before replacing the wallet back inside his left sock.

Newman did remember Rabin. Not only because of his accent but also, because of his short black beard. He was one of the physicians who came to listen to Peter Rooney. But Phil had never heard of a New Haven Jewish Hospital. He would have to look it up on the Internet later.

After his last case of the day, a thoracotomy, Philip remained in the post anesthesia care unit until he was sure that the patient was able to open his eyes and could be extubated.

This male patient was muscular and strong. The only reason why he was not able to remove the tube from his windpipe by himself, was because his hands were still attached with wrist cuffs, to the bedside rails. But his non-stop efforts were good indications of a normal recovery. After deflating the endotracheal balloon surrounding the tube, Newman removed the adhesive tape gluing the tube to the cheeks. During the extubation, he suctioned the copious secretions from the trachea and the pharynx. The surgeon was busy checking the chest tube which drained unimpeded, into a large plastic bag. Everything was OK. The doctors agreed to leave, for the time being, the patient's wrists attached to the bed, to prevent him from pulling on the chest tube.

With his endotracheal tube removed, the patient was now able to talk. In a hoarse voice, he began to complain of pains. The anesthesiologist administered a smaller first dose of painkiller directly into the intravenous infusion tubing, after which he left written orders for more medications: *Demerol 75 mgms IM. Q 4 H, PRN for pains.*

thirty-nine

It was just before 4:30 in the afternoon when Philip parked the car in his garage. Kyra was not home yet. He made himself a cup of coffee and, coffee in hand, went to his den to check the answering machine. Its light blinked, sign that there was a new message. It was Ethan Rabin again. He wanted Dr. Newman to know that because of a cancellation and, at patient's insistence, the tattoo removal had been rescheduled for an earlier date. It will take place in one week, first case in the morning.

He repeated his home phone number.

Without wasting a second, Philip called Peter Rooney's cell phone. The FBI agent answered after 3 rings: "Pete speaking."

"Hi, Pete, this is Phil. Phil Newman. I have a case for us." Philip transmitted the messages received, including the change of schedule.

"Very interesting Phil. They seem to be in a hurry. I wonder why."

"I wonder, too. It will be a week from today, first case in the morning."

"What time?"

"Good question, Pete. In most hospitals the first incision is made at 7:30. Rarely at 8.:00 You know what? Assume it's 7:30. I'll call you back if it's not. Are you going to be able to come?"

"Of course, Doc. I'll try to get a flight to Bradley Airport. And you?"

"I'll drive. I'll book space for me and my car on the ferry to Connecticut. Do you want me to pick you up at Bradley?"

"So early in the morning? Thank you for the offer, but don't bother. I'll arrange a Bureau car. And you don't have to call me back if there are only minor time changes. I will meet you in the main lobby of the New Haven Jewish at 7 o'clock in the morning, no matter what. Please do call if the changes are major."

"Aye-aye, Sir!"

Before he returned Rabin's call, Philip had to check with Edward Morris, to make sure that he could have the day off, a week from today. The curious chief of anesthesia listened to all the details. "No problem, Phil. I wish you luck. I hope your theory will be proven correct."

After booking a place on the first morning ferry, after printing the *MapQuest* directions to the New Haven Jewish Hospital and after checking the *Anesthesiology Web Page*, Phil Newman called Mike Rooney to bring him up-to-date. By the time Kyra arrived, Philip was too excited and too impatient to wait for her to cook. They went out for pizza and beer.

As requested, Philip returned Ethan Rabin's call the same evening, soon after their return from the Pizzeria Florentine. The New Haven physician answered immediately. Yes, the case was booked for 7:30. He was in charge with the anesthesia for the tattoo removal and therefore, would not be able to come down to escort them to the OR suite.. A nurse will be sent and meet them in the main lobby.

Being careful no to disclose too much, Phil needed to be sure that Rabin understood what would happen. "You're allowed to start the IV, attach the patient to monitors and, if the surgeon gets impatient, give permission to a nurse to start prepping the surgical site. That's all. But, please, and this is very important, don't give any medications without our permission. No narcotics, no tranquilizers, no Propofol, no Ketamine, no nothing. Also make sure that you obtain from your administration two passes to allow us to observe the case. And another thing: under any circumstances don't disclose that there is an investigation going on. If anyone questions who Peter Rooney is, say he's a pharmaceutical rep."

"Don't worry, Dr. Newman. I served in the Israeli army and I worked a couple of times with the boys from Shin Beth and Mossad, the Israeli Secret Services. I know how to keep my mouth shut."

"I'm not worried at all. But please tell me a few things about the surgeon. What kind of a guy is he? Would he buy a story about a defective monitoring device causing a delay?"

"Dr. Henry is a young surgeon and very much into electronics. He knows monitoring machines better than most of us. He has the latest contraptions in his office, slash outpatient surgery center. A defective monitor would be a tough sell."

"We'll let Peter Rooney handle him then. It is critical that the patient does not get suspicious about the delay."

"No problem, Dr. Newman. I'm glad to help, especially if it will reduce these damn malpractice fraud cases."

Newman liked this sincere fellow. He ended the call with "Thank you for your help, Dr. Rabin. It was nice talking to you. See you soon. Should I say goodbye or shalom?"

"Shalom, Doctor Newman."

forty

Since September 11 2001, travelers were required to arrive at the ferry terminal forty five minutes before departure, to allow time for security inspection. Such an early hour did not pose a problem for Newman. The man was used to waking up early, and continue going, going, going a day and a night. The only difference was that this time, rather than leave his home in green OR scrubs, he put on a suit, a clean shirt and a tie.

The ferry terminal clock showed 4:10 when he drove on the embarkation dock. It was a dark early morning. The so-called *security inspection* was a joke. It reminded Phil of an old comedian who claimed that a paranoid person who doesn't trust airport inspections, as a safety precaution, always carries a bomb on the plane. It is all a statistical matter. You have a risky one in a million chance to find yourself on an aircraft in which one crazy guy carries a bomb but, a much safer one in a trillion possibility, to be on an aircraft in which two crazy guys have a bomb each.

An hour later, the boat, cars and passengers were crossing the Long Island Sound. They reached the Connecticut shore without a hitch..

MapQuest was accurate. Phil had no problem finding the New Haven Jewish Hospital. It was 5 minutes after 7 o'clock when Newman locked his car in the visitor parking lot. Peter Rooney was already in the main lobby, chatting with a woman dressed in a white coat over green garb and with a paper cap on her head. Surely an OR nurse.

"Sorry for being late," said Philip, shaking hands.

Peter ignored the apologies. "Dr. Newman, please meet Irene Jones, nurse anesthetist. Miss Jones, this is Dr. Newman, anesthesiologist."

The nurse anesthetist provided them with visitor ID tags which they clipped to their lapels, before following her to the OR suite. Outside the operating suite, Irene pointed to the external entrance door of men's locker room. They immediately entered and changed the civilian clothes for surgical greens.

When they came out through the internal door, Irene Jones was there waiting. She examined them for a second and sent them back. They had forgotten the ID's. On their reappearance, with the plastic cards attached to their pockets, she gave each of them a paper mask. With their faces now covered, they followed her to room three. It was 7:26 in the morning.

A young man was already supine on the OR table with an intravenous infusion and a blood pressure cuff on the right arm. The left arm was out on a sterile armboard, its giant tattoo covered in iodine. All other monitoring devices were already in place. Scrubbed, gowned and gloved, the surgeon was standing a few feet away from the patient with his arms up, visibly impatient and annoyed.

Rabin spoke first. "Dr. Henry, please meet Dr. Newman, an anesthesiologist and Mr. Peter Rooney."

The surgeon spoke in a loud voice. "You better not think that I'm going to say nice to meet you! Who the hell are you? Why in the world was I not allowed to start my case before you arrived? What's going on?"

Peter Rooney replied calmly, "Please step outside Dr. Henry. I will explain everything."

The FBI agent left the operating room through the same door he entered. Furious, the surgeon threw his rubber gloves on the floor and followed Rooney out of the room. On his way out he muttered, "You better have a good explanation!"

The anesthesiologists remained in the room, with the patient and two nurses. Newman inquired, "May I see his medical history Dr. Rabin?" The patient's record passed from one anesthesiologist to the other. Phil turned toward the patient. "Your name is Aaron Aziz?"

Struggling to sit up, Aaron Aziz shouted, "Who the hell are you to read my chart?" Rabin checked the restraining straps to make sure the patient was safely tied down.

"My name is Dr. Philip Newman, I'm an anesthesiologist and I'd like to ask you a few questions, Mr. Aziz. First question, in what country did you get this tattoo?"

"None of your damn business! Just put me to sleep now!" On the electro-cardioscope, the heart rhythm was getting faster. Normal occurrence during excitement.

"We can't start the operation until you answer a few simple questions, Mr. Aziz. In what country did you get this tattoo?"

"Fuck you, stinking Jew! Put me to sleep now!" Aaron Aziz was shouting louder and louder. Unaware of what was going on, the two nurses looked at each other, puzzled.

"Mr. Aziz, if you have nothing to hide, why do you fight me instead of answering my question?"

"My chest is beginning to hurt! I'm going to die! Put me to sleep! PUT ME TO SLEEP!"

"Why do you think you're going to die? We didn't give you any medications yet."

"I know I'm going to die, I feel it! Put me to sleep!"

The EKG began to show some premature ventricular contractions.

For Newman it was *déjà vu*. The James Walker case all over again.

Ethan Rabin shouted, "PVC's ! Call *Code Blue*! Bring in the crash cart!"

Philip Newman acquiesced. "Bring in the cart. It probably won't help, but let's try CPR anyhow."

Dr. Henry and Peter Rooney followed the crash cart into the room. The patient was now unresponsive. He started to convulse and foam at the mouth. The tracing on the cardioscope quickly changed from PVC's to a bigemini rhythm, followed by ventricular fibrillation. Newman and Rabin followed the ABCs of human resuscitation to no avail. Aaron Aziz went into cardiac arrest before any anesthetic sedation was given. This was probably the reason why Aziz had convulsions and Walker didn't.

After pronouncing his patient dead, Dr. Henry shook the hands of the anesthesiologists and then put his arms on Peter Rooney's shoulders. "Thank you guys, it is hard to believe what just happened here. I owe you one! I need to go inform the family."

Rooney shrugged his shoulders. "They will most likely say they don't want an autopsy for religious reasons. But we will get a court order to ensure there is a post mortem examination."

The surgeon threw his paper cap in the hamper and left the room.

forty-one

It was early evening on the first Monday in February. As the telephone rang, Kyra shouted from the kitchen, "Could you please answer, honey? I'm busy!"

"No problem, baby." Phil picked up the receiver. "Newman residence."

"Hi Phil. Pete Rooney here."

"Hi Pete. How are you? Any news?"

"I wanted to find out if you are pleased with the results of the autopsy."

"Results? What results? I've heard nothing yet. The doctor is always the last to know."

Peter continued in a laughing voice, "Still paranoid, Doc? I think this will cure you. You were 100% right! Here are the post-mortem findings, '...a smell of almonds upon opening the gastric pouch...fragments of plastic capsule found in the stomach...and the toxicology exam showed Potassium Cyanide.'"

"Wow! Suicide by Potassium Cyanide. Just like Hermann Goring at the Nuremberg trial! The only difference was probably the plastic. I don't think it was invented yet during Hitler's era. If I remember well, the nazi bit into a glass vial which held the poison."

"Interesting historical information, Doc. I will have to check on that. Anyhow, we are now informing all the hospitals, all the physicians and all the medical liability insurers. Tomorrow, the news will hit the media."

"Fantastic! Does Mike know?"

"Not yet. I called you first."

"Thanks a million, Pete. Let me call him. Do you mind?"

"Be my guest."

Phil practically slammed the phone down and ran to tell Kyra the good news. Before she could even congratulate him, he grabbed the phone and pushed his speed dial for Los Angeles. Mike Rooney answered. On hearing the account, he became as excited as Newman. "Are you going to celebrate, Phil? I know I am!"

Philip thought for a second. "You know what, Mike? We should celebrate together. I promised Kyra a long time ago a visit to California. Why not do it now? I'll book a hotel. Could you please reserve a table for four in a good restaurant for next Saturday night?"

"French?"

"French? MMMMM ! French would be great!"

"Consider it done! See you soon.. Give my love to Kyra."

"Bye, Mike. Pass along the good news to Rita. And don't forget to kiss her hand for me."

"Always continental, Doctor Newman."

forty-two

It was Saturday night in Los Angeles when Phil and Kyra Newman joined Mike and Rita Rooney at their table for four at La Cachette. The waiter had only just finished pouring the wine, but Phil was itching to share with the Rooneys the news he learned hours earlier during the flight. He stood up ceremoniously, a glass of Heineken in his right hand. "My friends, lets us drink. Wine for the Rooneys, mineral water for my wife. We have some beautiful news. We are expecting a beautiful baby. Kyra is beautiful, Rita is beautiful and, as a matter of fact, we are all beautiful. This restaurant is beautiful, life is beautiful, the world is beautiful and, believe it or not, even the practice of anesthesia is now beautiful again!

Mike Rooney was in a teasing mood. "And what makes you, my dear doctor, such an expert on beauty?"

"Of course you wine drinkers have no idea what I'm talking about. I'm the only one here who knows beauty when I see it." Philip lifted his glass as high as he could and continued, "I will just repeat what I saw on a T-shirt of a Harley-Davidson biker: *BEAUTY IS IN THE EYES OF THE BEER HOLDER!*"

As soon as Kyra, Rita and Mike stopped laughing, the California anesthesiologist stood up and, with his wine glass in his hand, retorted in a serious voice. "In my humble opinion, Phil is 100% right about our wives, probably right about life and possibly right about everything else, with one exception: our profession. Since the day this chain of lawsuits started, I have more and more doubts about the future of Anesthesiology."

Rita, Kyra, and Philip looked at each other and quickly decided to forbid all other comments on the professional subject. Doctor Michael Rooney had no choice but obey.

The rest of the evening was pleasant.

Epilogue

The flight to New York was calm and their arrival to Long Island brought the daily life, back to normal. The *jet lag* was minimal and it didn't stop Newman from covering a busy anesthesia call the next day. It was about 72 hours since the return home, when Philip finally found the time to check his email. After erasing spam, he opened the only one real letter. It was from Rooney. It said, "Dear Phil. Thank you for the fantastic time we had together. Please read my latest blog on the *Anesthesiology Web Page* and give me your unbiased opinion. All our love to you and Kyra from both of us."

Philip found the web page he was looking for on the Internet history and clicked on it, without closing the mail file. Mike's methinks were on the main page:

"A Little surgery for The Hippocratic Oath.

By Michael Rooney MD

I was brought up mono. Religion: monotheistic. Romantic inclinations: monogamous. Favorite game: Monopoly. My school life was monotonous. Good preparation for medical studies full of monomers, monopods, monomorphes, mononuclears and mononucleosis. Then came graduation. We were handed copies of a printed monologue: "THE HIPPOCRATIC OATH" and instructed to swear on a bunch of Greek gods and goddesses. And I remember asking myself: what happened to the good old monotheism?

Here we are in the modern nuclear age, surrounded by hungry ambulance chasers ready to destroy a noble profession in the name of the all-mighty dollar and they still make brand new physicians take the same vow, written about 400 years before the birth of Jesus Christ. Do you remember it?

The Hippocratic Oath.

I SWEAR: by Apollo the physician, by Æsculapius, Hygeia, and Panacea, and I take to witness all the gods, all the goddesses, to keep according to my ability and my judgment, the following Oath:

To consider dear to me as my parents him who taught me this art; to live in common with him and if necessary to share my goods with him; to look upon his children as my own brothers, to teach them this art if they so desire without fee or written promise; to impart to my sons and the sons of the master who taught me and the disciples who have enrolled themselves and have agreed to the rules of the profession, but to these alone the precepts and the instruction.

I will prescribe regimen for the good of my patients according to my ability and my judgment and never do harm to anyone. To please no one will I prescribe a deadly drug nor give advice which may cause his death. Nor will I give a woman a pessary to procure abortion. But I will preserve the purity of my life and my art. I will not cut for stone, even for patients in whom the disease is manifest; I will leave this operation to be performed by practitioners, specialists in this art.

In every house where I come I will enter only for the good of my patients, keeping myself far from all intentional ill-doing and all seduction and especially from the pleasures of love with women or with men, be they free or slaves. All that may come to my knowledge in the exercise of my profession or in daily commerce with men, which ought not to be spread abroad, I will keep secret and will never reveal.

If I keep this oath faithfully, may I enjoy my life and practice my art, respected by all men and in all times; but if I swerve from it or violate it, may the reverse be my lot.

Let me now ask you: is this acceptable in the 21st Century? I don't think so. In my professional opinion, in our days, the Hippocratic Oath is totally obsolete. What do my web readers think? Here is my revised version, adapted—of course—to its ancient original style, for your comments and/or approval:

The Non-Hypocritic Oath

I swear:

To **obey** the law and practice medicine to the best of my knowledge and according to my local judges, medical malpractice lawyers, jury decisions, mandatory second opinions, liability insurance companies and HMO limitations.

If abortions remain legal, I will or I will not produce them, depending on my own personal beliefs, on the number of abortion clinics burned in my immediate vicinity, and on the number of anti-abortion people picketing the local hospitals.

I will give no deadly medicine to anyone if asked, nor suggest any such counsel. Unless, of course, a euthanasia law is finally passed and I will then make such desperate decisions case by case.

Whatever in connection with my professional practice, or not in connection with it, I see or hear, in the life of men or women which ought not to be spoken of here or abroad, I will not divulge, as reckoning that all such should be kept secret.

Unless of course, their charts are subpoenaed by medical liability attorneys, requested by Medicare or Medicaid, checked by the hospital peer review committees or investigated by the department of Health.

While I continue to keep this Oath unviolated, may it be granted to me to enjoy life and the practice of the Art of Defensive Medicine.

With one push of computer button, Newman returned to the mail file. His answer to Rooney read:

Dear Mike.
You're a very good and convincing writer. After reading your blog my *being a doctor* pessimism has totally returned. Now I have bad news and worse news.
The bad news? If You are right, the end of the medical profession as we know it, is just around the corner.
The worse news? YOU'RE RIGHT !

As is the custom in email between friends, Philip Newman did not bother to sign his name before pressing *send.*

THE END.

Printed in the United States
100293LV00002B/190-231/A